The
Weigher of
Souls
&
The
Earth
Dwellers

ANDRÉ MAUROIS

Autobiographical Introduction
Epilogue by Jacques Choron
Translated by Hamish Miles
Illustrated by Leonard Everett Fisher

The Weigher of Souls

&

The Earth Dwellers

The Macmillan Company, New York

Library of Congress catalogue card number: 63-13325

The Macmillan Company, New York
A DIVISION OF THE CROWELL-COLLIER PUBLISHING COMPANY

First Printing

Printed in the United States of America

DESIGNED BY RONALD FARBER

Contents

List of Illustrations

Autobiographical
Introduction

In the
Twilight
of My Life

I WAS BORN in Elbeuf, a small French industrial town, on July 26, 1885. My father was a textile manufacturer; my mother, a highly cultured woman, gave me my early education. I used to listen with delight as she read aloud from the great poets, and I decided, when I was eight or nine, that I would one day be a writer—a most unlikely decision since the more natural course would have been to succeed my father. Yet, at the age of ten, I wrote a verse tragedy in five acts. It must have been very bad, and was, fortunately lost during the Second World War.

Elbeuf being in Normandy, Rouen was our capital town, and I was sent there to the *lycée* (a French high school). My first teacher said: "Yes, you will be a writer." And, at the end of the year, he gave me a book of Russian short stories containing work by the nineteenth-century writers Alexander Pushkin, Nikolai Gogol, and others. On the flyleaf he wrote: "I want you to remember your old master when you publish your first book." That gave me some hope.

A few years later, another teacher became an important influence on me. I met Émile Auguste Chartier, one of the greatest professors of philosophy, who wrote under the name of Alain and who was soon to become justly famous. Two fine French writers of the nineteenth century, Honoré de Balzac and Stendahl (Marie Henri Beyle), were his favorite authors. They became, and still are, mine.

My ambition was to teach philosophy and write books. Alain disagreed. "No," he said, "go and work with your father. An active life is the best way to know men. Balzac was a printer; Charles Dickens a reporter. If you have a real vocation, you will write anywhere." I trusted his judgment, but I went back to Elbeuf with a heavy heart. I did not know anybody in the world of letters; the publishing houses were all located in Paris and seemed totally out of my reach. Moreover, I was not quite happy with my tentative writings. I had read so many great books that I could tell a poor one. But I kept on hoping and spent my evenings reading and writing.

In 1914 the First World War began. Much to my surprise, and because I could more or less speak

English, I was attached to the British Army. I had spent many a holiday in England and greatly admired English literature—the poets, and also Jonathan Swift, Laurence Sterne, and Charles Dickens. I got on well with my British brother officers. They seemed to me so different from the traditional image given, in France, of an Englishman that I began a book about them. By 1917, it was completed; I called it *The Silences of Colonel Bramble (Les Silences du Colonel Bramble)*. I knew it was not too bad but did not think it possible to have it published. I did not even try.

Luckily, we had with us another French officer who was a Parisian and the friend of a young and enterprising publisher to whom he offered to submit my manuscript. It was accepted, printed at the beginning of 1918, and was received amazingly well by both the critics and the public. A hundred thousand copies were sold immediately in France and many in England. Some of the writers I admired, Rudyard Kipling, Anatole France, and André Gide corresponded with me about the book. Also, Georges Clemenceau, who was then the French Prime Minister, wrote: "Come and see me after the war." I was astonished. It was like a tale from the *Thousand and One Nights*. One day, I had brooded sadly over my wasted life; the next morning, I awoke to find myself the writer of a bestseller. I could hardly believe it.

When the war was over, I told my father I wanted to leave the family business and devote myself entirely to writing; he was very kind and understanding about my decision and did not object. I wrote one more book about the war and *Ariel,* the life of Shelley, which was published in America. Then, in 1930 I was asked to lecture in the United States; Princeton University offered me a chair of French literature, which I accepted, and for one year my old dream of teaching came true. I immensely enjoyed my year at Princeton and visited America five times between the two world wars.

During these years I wrote a number of books. Some were biographies, among them *Byron, Chateaubriand,* and *Disraeli,* which was chosen by the Book of the Month Club. Others were novels: *Bernard Quesnay, Climates (Climats), The Family Circle (Le Cercle de Famille).* Strangely enough, in France I was better known as a novelist while in America and England my fiction met with little success and my biographies did well. One exception was the story published in 1931 and reprinted hereafter, *The Weigher of Souls (Le Peseur d'Âmes).* I was very fond of fantastic tales. The English writer H. G. Wells had become a friend of mine, and also a young English novelist, David Garnett. I had translated (for publication in France) his *Lady into Fox;* he returned the compliment by translating, admirably, *The Weigher of Souls.*

The idea of that story, entirely imaginary, had come to me during the First World War. Many of my friends and relatives having then been killed, it was perhaps natural that my thoughts turned to death. About that time, I read, in some newspaper, two lines about a mad physician who weighed bodies after death, but it took a long time (seven or eight years) before the idea took shape. Then one day, in London, I met an English doctor who was exactly the type I needed, and with this impetus the book was written in two weeks. Many readers took it seriously. Even now, I still sometimes receive a letter or a cable, from a faraway country saying, "Is *The Weigher of Souls* a true story?" I did do my best to make it credible and even asked the greatest French physicist of the time, Jean Perrin, to design the scientific apparatus, which he did with enjoyment and care.

As to the other story in this volume, *The Earth Dwellers,* the idea came to me while I was reading the wonderful book on insect life written by the great French entomologist of the nineteenth century Jean Henri Fabre. He described some extraordinary feats performed by insects and kept on warning the reader: "Do not believe there is any intelligence in all that. It's just instinct. Bees have no patriotism with regard to the bee hive nor ants toward the anthill."

Suddenly the idea flashed into my mind that, if giant beings from other planets observed *us,* they would probably come to the same conclusion. "Do not believe," they might say, "that men love their wives or their children. They cannot even distinguish between them and other women or children." I saw at once that the subject lent itself to Swiftian remarks and to a satire of hastily drawn conclusions.

In 1938 I was elected to the French Academy. It seemed as if the game of life was won. It was not. The following year the Second World War began. I volunteered as an officer and was again attached to the British Army. I hoped that I might be able to find material to write "The Grandson of Colonel Bramble, or Twenty Years After," but events turned out more tragically. In May 1940, I advanced with the British into Belgium and was caught in the great retreat. After many adventures, I managed to cross the German lines and return to Paris. From there, the French General Staff sent me to London where I was demobilized. The year before, Europe being then at peace, I had promised to give the Lowell Lectures in Boston in October of 1940. I was now able to fulfill this promise and crossed over to Canada in a British ship where I rejoined my wife, who had succeeded in reaching Lisbon and then flying to Montreal. We then went straight to Boston.

I could not possibly go back to occupied France— I was Jewish-born and also had written many articles against Hitler—so I stayed in America. For two successive summers, I lived in California, at Mills College. There we had created a Maison Française, a center for French studies, where Darius Milhaud taught music; Fernand Leger, painting; and I, literature. After that, I lectured in many universities.

During this time I wrote several books: *Tragedy in France* (*Tragédie en France*); *I Remember, I Remember* (*Memoires*), a volume of memoirs; and a *History of the United States* (*Histoire des États-Unis*).

When I was not away lecturing, I lived in New York, where we had found many of our European friends, among them the French writers Antoine de Saint-Exupery and Jules Romains, the Belgian writer Maurice Maeterlinck, the German novelist and essayist Thomas Mann, and the Austrian writer Stefan Zweig, who soon left for Brazil, where he committed suicide. American writers and editors were very kind to us and I was able to publish articles in *The New York Times, Life, The Saturday Review of Literature* and other periodicals. I had to make a living, for my wife and I had arrived without a cent.

In 1942, when the United States entered the war and the American troops landed in North Africa, I volunteered once more and went to Algiers, as a French captain, on an American transport. I was the only Frenchman aboard and (aged fifty-seven) much older than American captains. A naval officer came to me and asked: "Excuse me, sir, but are you a mere captain? You are so old. . . . You ought to be a general." I agreed, but the fact remained, I was just a captain. "Well, sir," he said, "I'll put you with the generals; you'll be more comfortable."

From Algiers, I went to Tunisia and later to

Corsica; then I joined General Juin in Italy. It is a curious fact that though I was never a professional soldier, I spent eight years of my life in the army. I even wrote a book of *Dialogues* on military leadership. One doesn't plan one's life.

When my wife and I returned to France in 1946, I found that my library and most of my furniture had been stolen, so we had to make a new beginning. I worked very hard and never produced more books than between my sixtieth and seventieth years. Two novels, *Woman without Love* (*Terre Promise*) and *September Roses* (*Les Roses de Septembre*), a history of France (*Histoire de la France*), and a volume of short stories, *For Solo Piano* (*Pour Piano Seul*). My principal work was biography, and among the volumes at this time are biographies of the French writers Marcel Proust, *Remembrance of Marcel Proust* (*Á la Recherche de Marcel Proust*), George Sand (*Lélia*), Victor Hugo (*Olympio*), and Alexandre Dumas, father and son (*The Titans*).

One of the biographies I wrote surprised my friends very much; it was a *Life of Sir Alexander Fleming* (*La Vie de Sir Alexander Fleming*), the inventor of penicillin. "Why a scientist?" people asked me. "It does not seem to be your field." As a matter of fact, I have always been deeply interested in science; in this case, the suggestion had come from Lady Fleming, the widow of the great man. She flew to Paris in 1955 and told me, "I want you to write the life of my husband; I shall place all his papers at your disposal." I said, "I feel very grateful, Lady

Fleming, but I know very little about bacteriology."
"You will learn," she answered.

So I spent six months in a laboratory at the Pasteur Institute and did learn enough to write the book. I greatly enjoyed that experience; it taught me a great deal about the principles of scientific research and, moreover, Fleming was a character after my own heart, a taciturn Scot like the Colonel Bramble of my first book. I thought at one time of calling his life "The Silences of Professor Fleming." It did not sound respectful enough; yet I sometimes regret having given it up. It would have looped the loop of a long literary career.

At the time of this writing, I am in my seventy-eighth year and again engaged in a long and difficult book. Moreover, I keep in my files quite a number of projects: novels, biographies, essays. Will they ever get written? Most of them certainly not. And why work so much when so few years are left to one and when rest seems well earned? My friend and fellow countryman and writer, François Mauriac says, "Anyway, our paper has now been handed over to the Examiner. One more book will make no difference." It is true. Yet he goes on writing and so do I. Why? First from sheer delight and also because of the secret hope to create at last, in the twilight of my life, the mysterious and wonderful book I dreamed of when, as a child, I listened to my mother reading aloud from the masters.

André Maurois

The
Weigher of
Souls

The

Weigher of

Souls

I

I HAVE HESITATED a long time before setting
down this story. I am aware that it will astonish those
who have been dearest to me, and be distasteful to
more than one of them. Some will doubt my good
faith, others my good sense. My own thoughts would
have been the same had I not been the accidental,
and protesting, eyewitness of the facts I am about to
relate. So conscious am I of their apparent absurdity
that I have never mentioned them even to my closest
intimates. And if my mind is now made up to break
this silence, it is because I do not feel that I have
the right to leave to destruction after my own death
the sole object remaining as evidence of this strange
dream.

Before my readers reject Dr. James's theories as altogether improbable, I would ask them to recall what I believe to have been the extreme cautiousness of my mind. Like all men I have had my passions and weaknesses; I have tried to safeguard my judgment. In science, in metaphysics, in politics, and even in my sentimental life, I have made a point of never mistaking my wishes for proofs. I am far from having always succeeded, but perhaps that constant circumspection will be counted in my favor at a moment when I shall stand in every need of credence.

There is a second argument in my favor: the facts I have to narrate are surprising, but their nature is not impossible to verify. A few simple experiments, which can be easily repeated by any physicist, biologist, or doctor, will show that James's theories, even if they are regarded as absurd, were based upon actual observations. Why did I not continue these experiments myself? Why have I not made them known until after my death? It is not very easy for me to explain. The main factor, I think, was shyness, together with a natural distaste for occupying myself with certain problems. Circumstances had made me a writer, not a scientist. I had access to neither a hospital nor a laboratory. I was reluctant to get into touch with men to whom I was one of the profane, in order that I might draw their attention to phenomena which, as I knew, would contradict their ideas. I regret my weakness; and I should be happy if the publication of this memoir were to inspire in

some adventurous minds a desire to follow my hapless friend in the exploration of a new world, the
knowledge of which might well lead to results of
great significance.

*   *   *

I knew Dr. James during the War. We first met in
a muddy Flanders field, and amid a group of cheerful and healthy Englishmen his gaunt, prominent
cheekbones and the look of torment on his face at
once impressed me. He had been attached to the
medical services of the division with which I served
as French liaison officer. We immediately became
friendly, and notwithstanding the horror of those
days and scenes, the months which I spent in the
Ypres Salient in his company left me with memories
that might almost be termed enjoyable. Between our
two camp beds a packing case served as table and
library. At night, when sleep was denied us by the
shells screaming their way overhead toward Poper-
inghe and the clacking of the soaked canvas in the
wind, we held muttered converse about madmen
and poets. I liked my companion. Beneath his casing
of cynicism I caught glimpses of the bold and tender
spirit within. So reticent was he that I shared his
daily life for months on end without knowing
whether he had either wife or children.

The armistice cut short this friendship, as it did
so many others. For a year we exchanged letters, and

I thus learned that James was on the staff of one of the London hospitals. Then one of us (which, I couldn't now say) failed to answer a letter. James became an image still entangled with my memories, but an unreal image, like that of a character in a novel. And in the end I ceased to think about him, even in dream, until the spring of 1925.

During that year I had occasion to stay a long while in London for some research at the British Museum. I was there alone, rather tired and depressed by too much continuous work. One morning the sunshine was so bright that I did not have the courage to immure myself in the reading room. For a moment or two I stood watching the pigeons under the Greek colonnade of the museum, as friendly and as distant as those of Saint Mark's. I stood in a brown study. The realization was forced on me that solitude, healthy enough for a short time, was becoming intolerable. Yet I did not lack English friends—why hadn't I tried to look them up? Wouldn't it be pleasant to spend the evenings with such an intelligent fellow as Dr. James? I had forgotten his address, but it is never hard to trace a doctor; and entering the reading room, I discovered from a medical directory that H. B. James, M.D., was on the resident staff of Saint Barnaby's Hospital. I decided to drop my work for that morning, and to go and hunt up my friend.

Saint Barnaby's Hospital lies south of the Thames, in the crowded region that stretches beyond Blackfriars Bridge. To cross the river thereabouts always impresses me in a strange and compelling way. The Thames there is the frontier of two worlds. One leaves the Gothic and Renaissance London, the London of chessboard squares, of the tree-lined embankments beneath the great hotels, of the red stream of buses, for a city of factories and warehouses, bare walls, and blunt chimney stacks. And the contrast that morning struck me the more forcibly as, just when I was crossing the bridge, a great cloud suddenly obscured the sun. In a gloomy, stormy light I reached the slime-covered bank side where men were loading stranded barges with sacks of cement. Along the thoroughfare roared the metallic din of tram cars and steam tractors. Alongside the pavement seethed a wretched street market. I was entering the territory of a different people.

A policeman told me how to reach Saint Barnaby's. Situated on the river's edge, the hospital seemed to me like a refuge amid all the sordid houses and the blind walls of warehouses. Like so many London buildings, it resembled one of those edifices in romantic engravings, with long white streaks emphasizing the black violence of the shadows, but it was enlivened here and there by little splashes of vivid color—the green of turf, the lavender-blue uniform of a nurse, the bright red dressing gowns of three convalescents taking their first stroll. Above the iron gates a large streamer displayed an inscription to the effect that Saint Barnaby's was supported by voluntary contributions, and that at the present moment there was a deficit of thirty thousand pounds. I entered and asked the porter whether Dr. H. B. James was attached to the hospital.

"Dr. James?" he said. "Certainly, sir. . . . At this time you'll probably find him in the residents' lodge. . . . Straight under the memorial arch, and first on your left."

I obeyed, and found a small detached block, likewise of smoke-blackened white stone, but covered with ivy and Virginia creeper. A board at the foot of the stairs showed the names of the doctors, each of them followed by the indication "IN" or "OUT." At the top of the list I read: "DR. H. B. JAMES, 1ST FLOOR, ROOM 21. IN." I went up and found my friend's name inscribed on the wooden plate of one of the doors. Then suddenly I felt anxious—in fact, almost shy. Would he be pleased at seeing me after such long oblivion? Should I merely find myself alone again, after a few polite remarks, in that dismal cluster of chimneys and slums? I knocked, and with an unconscious movement took hold of the door-knob. It did not turn. It seemed to be held fast from within. A voice, that once-familiar grating voice that seemed torn by the wind from rusted scrap iron, came in what struck me as a dry tone:

"Just one moment, please."

In the ensuing silence I heard hasty footsteps, the noise of sliding rings from a hurriedly pulled curtain, a squeal rather like that of a small animal pinched or hit by mistake, and then a clinking of glasses being thrown against each other. Water flowed into a basin, gentle and irritating. Standing in front of the door I waited, vaguely uneasy. What was James doing? Had I interrupted some operation, a dressing, an examination? It seemed unlikely. James was not a surgeon, and in any case he would not have brought a patient to his own room. Was he rising late after being on night duty? Had I wakened him? At last the water ceased, steps came toward me, the doorknob turned beneath my hand, and through the half-opened door I saw the doctor's head. He was even more gaunt than during the War. His eyes, with deep hollows beneath the orbits, shone with a troubled and, as it were, veiled gleam; in the expression there was something haggard which I found extremely painful. For a moment he hesitated before picking on the exact memory that fitted his unexpected caller, then smiled and opened the door wide. I saw that he was wearing a white coverall.

"Hullo, my boy! What the deuce are *you* doing in England? You're the last person I'd have expected to see this morning!"

The room was simply furnished: a camp bed, two chairs, a big leather armchair, and a few shelves, some laden with books, the rest hidden by a green canvas curtain, the same one, no doubt, that I had heard sliding on its rod. In one corner stood a hand basin full of soapy water; on the mantelpiece, several photographs of a young woman. James offered me

the armchair and handed me a cigarette box, but he kept looking around with an air of such anxiety that I wondered if there could be a third person hidden in the room. Then he made an effort to talk, with just the air of feigned interest that might be assumed by one interrupted in some dubious occupation and trying to assume ease of manner.

"Well, well!" he said. "You certainly seem to have dropped me since you became an historian. . . . I read that last book of yours, although you didn't send me it. . . . Not bad. I shouldn't have thought you had it in you. . . . But books apart, what's been happening to you?"

I had arrived full of pleasure at seeing again a man of whom I had been fond, a man, too, who had given me some of my keenest intellectual enjoyment. But I felt vexed and so ill at ease that my pleasure was completely spoiled. I saw that James and I had almost nothing to say to each other. We had known each other as members of a group which had long ceased to exist. Of our 1918 soul, nothing survived. Our common anguish regarding the outcome of the War, our common affection for wounded friends, were sentiments as dead as the superficial cells which had then formed our earthly framework. To the self who had just entered this room, the James who dwelt there was a being almost as completely a stranger as any random passer-by I might have stopped in Piccadilly. I felt that the only way of again reaching the deeper and more stable layers in him was to confess my disappointment.

"It's an odd thing, James," I said, "but do you remember an evening of ours at Ypres when you told me about the dissociation of personality in madness? I feel something very like that at this moment! I came to your room to find a Self which no longer exists, and I am vainly longing for the moment of madness that might allow me to be pleased at seeing you. . . ."

Such a remark would have sufficed to rouse the James I had once known to a discourse at once learned and humorous. But he shrugged his shoulders wearily, lit a cigarette, and sank into one of the chairs, still looking anxiously around.

"Ah, well!" he sighed. "It's a long time since I gave up worrying about dissociations and sublimations. . . . I look after people with cancer and heart disease and lung troubles. . . . The Port of London occasionally sends me compatriots of yours, seamen. . . ."

At that instant, from behind the green curtain, there came a sound that is never forgotten by any who have heard it—the scampering of a rat, a swift, dry sound accentuated by the hard claws of the feet. Suddenly I had visions of a dugout which I once shared with James in a railway cutting.

"Hullo!" I said laughingly. "Do you keep rats? That's something to stir up common memories for us!"

"Rats?" he said, rising with a look of displeasure. "How do you suppose there would be rats in a hos-

pital? You're suffering from hallucinations, my boy.
. . . I say, I'm awfully sorry, but we can't stay here.
. . . It's time for me to go round my wards. Would
you like to come with me? It might interest you."

I was now definitely embarrassed.

"Are you sure I shan't be in the way?" I said. "I
can easily come back some other time."

"No," he answered, in a tone of mingled good will
and irony. "No, you aren't in my way now. . . ."

He stepped quickly over to the sink, and taking a
little soapy water, wiped a red smear from the edge
of the basin.

II

Saint Barnaby's Hospital struck me as one of the
least gloomy that could be imagined. The floors of
the wards were tiled in black-and-white squares, the
red beds were trimly ranged, the windows had their
flowers; and oases of healthy freshness were set in this
realm of sickness by the nurses, almost all of them
pretty and kindly, in their blue print dresses. Each
ward was ruled over by a ward sister, recognizable by
the deeper blue of her belt.

"Nothing to report, sister?" James asked.

"I'd like you to have a look at number 216, doctor.
The fever's not going down. . . ."

He went over to the bed. Turning over the case
sheet hung above the patient's head, he made an

effort to remember the history of the illness, and ordered a change of treatment in a mournful, tired voice. In the women's ward, I was struck by his indifference. In myself the sight of a sick woman (especially if she be young and pleasing) has always inspired an ardent sense of pity, mingled perhaps with sensuality. I realized that a doctor entering these rooms would not, as I did, experience a sensation at once agonizing and grateful, a feeling of invaded intimacy and melting compassion; yet it surprised me to see how insensitive my companion was to the little blandishments of some of these dying women. There was one girl, deathly pale under her long, loosened hair, who attempted a smile as we passed, only to fall back upon her pillow, gasping for breath.

"Poor child!" I said to James.

"Which?" he said. "Oh, yes. . . . 318. No hope for her. . . ."

In the male wards several patients were out of bed, standing grouped in their red jackets round the beds or the flower-laden tables. There was a dock strike in progress at the time, and many of the patients were slightly injured men who stood there arguing politics and religion among themselves in the weighty tone of Hyde Park orators. I saw my friend's eyes soften as he spoke to one strikingly handsome lad of fifteen.

"Is that you, sonny?" he said. "No more giddiness? You can go out tomorrow. . . . Anything to report, sister?"

"I don't think 413 will get through the night, doctor. He doesn't open his eyes any longer."

James went over to a corner bed where an old man was lying. His thin cheeks and nostrils seemed to be sucked in toward the inside of his body. He was breathing very fast. His ruddy-white beard had not been shaved for several days. James took the sick man's pulse; he was unconscious and showed no reaction.

"You're right, sister," he said with sudden animation. "He won't last the night. . . . I'll warn Gregory. Don't bother about anything. . . . In any case I'll come in and see him during the day. Get him a little camphorated oil; it will keep him going until the evening."

I was taken aback by this sudden change in my friend. His excitement now seemed to equal his previous indifference.

"I must go and see the post-mortem clerk," he said. "Come along with me; that will interest you."

"What is the post-mortem clerk?" I asked.

"Forgotten your Latin? He's the assistant responsible for seeing to the autopsy of the corpse after a patient dies. Ours is a queer little man called Gregory."

We went down three flights of stairs. James pushed back a heavy door laden with bolts; and we entered an amphitheater capable of holding about twenty onlookers, the white walls coated with a shiny varnish, and with four dissecting tables in the center.

The air was impregnated with an unpleasant smell of formaldehyde. I gave a start when a small figure of a man seemed to rise with diabolic abruptness from the middle of the amphitheater. He repelled me from my first glimpse of him. And yet his appearance was quite commonplace, the points of his waxed mustache twisting spirally up toward his gold-rimmed glasses. When James mentioned this clerk of the corpses I had imagined, for some reason or other, a sort of romantic executioner; and I was shocked by this polite, tradesman-like vulgarity in conjunction with the idea of death.

"Morning, Gregory," said the doctor. "This is a French friend of mine who is going over the hospital. . . . I came in to warn you that we shall certainly have number 413 tonight."

"Very good, doctor," said the little man. "I'll come this evening. Everything will be ready. Ten o'clock?"

"Yes, about ten," said James. "A little earlier if you can."

"And by the way, doctor," asked Gregory in a lowered voice, "you aren't forgetting that you owe me for the last two?"

James looked all around with the same anxious glance that had surprised me in his room, and taking two notes from his wallet he handed them to Gregory. The latter eyed me through his spectacles.

"Perhaps," he said, slowly folding the notes, "the French gentleman would like to see our installation?"

I murmured some unintelligible remark. The

smell of this room was beginning to give me qualms, and I was afraid of making myself look foolish by fainting.

"Our organization," the little man went on complacently, "enables us to deal, in this room and that next door, with as many as eight corpses daily. It is quite enough—except in midsummer, because the babies crowd me up then. . . . And yet, sir, with methodical handling, even in the busy season, I can keep up. . . . can't I, doctor? I've done as many as four on the same table. . . . Feet here and head there. . . . Hard work, I can tell you! No, no, don't go this way out, sir. You haven't seen the best. . . ."

He turned toward the iron door let into the varnished wall, on which a notice was pasted: "*Professor Simpson wishes to have hearts intact. The greatest care must be taken.*" Bolts creaked. Slowly the door turned. I was caught by a sense of mortal chill. I must have been rather pale, for James took my arm and gave me a close look. Going down a few steps, we reached a large, brick-walled cellar. In the center of the refrigerating room stood a metal apparatus which looked like a baker's oven, a boiler, or more exactly, with its long projecting rods, a gigantic waffle iron. Gregory gave me a glance, signed to me with an air of hidden understanding as if he were on the point of giving me a wonderful present, and then, with remarkable agility, opened two doors, and pulled one of the rods. I almost cried out loud, for he had drawn forward to where we stood a long platform on which lay a naked woman.

How lovely she was, that dead creature! I shall never forget the unearthly whiteness of that body, on which the points of the breasts laid twin stains of pale pink. Her eyes were closed. A sad, lofty smile gave shape to a delicious mouth. How had such a woman come to die in an outlying hospital? One would have liked to know her, to console her, to help her. . . . Gregory and James stood motionless, eying me.

"Do you recognize her, doctor?" said Gregory. "It's that Russian girl. . . . They're waiting for the relatives to claim her. . . ."

He pushed back the rod with an abrupt jerk, thrusting platform and body into the black metal machine, and said with an air of pride:

"We can keep them indefinitely in this cold. . . . Would you like to see a man?"

"No, thanks," I said. "I'd like to get outside."

James took my arm again, kindly this time.

"I'll take you up to my room," he said, "and you shall have a glass of port. You don't look well. . . . And look, Gregory—is that fixed for this evening?"

At that moment a muffled bell sounded in the amphitheater: *tak-tak . . . tak-tak-tak-tak. . . .*

"Two-four," said Gregory. "That's for you, doctor."

"Excuse me," said James, "I must leave you for a moment. . . . Yes, we all have our own signals on these bells. Mine is two-four. . . . There are bells like that in every ward and in our rooms too. . . . All I have to do now is to telephone to the lodge, and they'll tell me where I'm needed. . . . You wait here for me."

"I'd rather see you somewhere else, doctor. Will you dine with me tonight? I'm staying in a delightful little hotel in the city. . . ."

"Tonight?" he murmured absently. . . . "Tonight? Yes, at a pinch, I can get someone to take my place. . . . I, too, should very much like to have a talk. Only you heard just now—I must be back at ten o'clock. If you're willing to dine early, about seven, I can come."

"I'll expect you. . . . Johnson's Hotel. . . ."

High up in the amphitheater the buzzer was repeating: *tak-tak, tak-tak-tak-tak*.

III

The proprietor of Johnson's Hotel prided himself on having installed neither central heating nor electric light; but a huge fire of logs blazed in the hall fireplace, silver candlesticks gleamed on the dining-room table, the servants were silent and respectful, and the visitor felt that to them he was not a number but a man. I asked the headwaiter to give me for this dinner the small private dining room; I liked its light oak paneling, and on coming in about seven o'clock, I was struck by a sense of surprising intimacy. On the mahogany of the table a vase of jonquils shone in the soft light of the candles. When James arrived a moment later, I noticed with pleasure that he too responded to the charming simplicity of the setting.

"Ah!" he said, standing warming his hands in front of the fire, "it takes a Frenchman to discover corners of old England in the middle of London. What a good idea of yours! I needed a rest so badly. . . . Strictly speaking, I don't deal with the outpatients, but the list is so heavy on Mondays that I give my colleagues a hand if I can."

"Why are there more patients on Monday?"

"Oh, that's easy enough! In our poor districts, Monday is the day when the rent-collector calls for the week's money. The women contrive not to be at home, and so as to have an excuse they bring their children along to us. You ought to see that someday; it's incredible! Some of them leave their brats on the benches and go for a drink at the pub opposite. After the consultation they have to be found and brought back, all drowsy with beer, and made to pick out one from the kids who've been left behind. . . . Besides, there are the Sunday accidents, fights, and, of course, my own patients. . . . It's a stiff day."

"Sit down, James. . . . We'll try to put the hospital out of your mind. Do you remember that Burgundy we used to drink at Amiens? I've ordered you the very same."

Wartime memories occupied us during the soup, and then James retired into an impregnable taciturnity. I remembered that he used often to emerge from such fits of abstraction with one of those dazzling, paradoxical speeches which had made me like him. So I remained silent myself, and waited.

"Tell me," he said suddenly. "There's one question I've never asked you. . . . even at times when it would have been very natural. Do you believe in the immortality of the soul?"

I was a little surprised, but quite pleased, for in this abrupt exordium I once more saw the James of my memories. I reflected for a moment.

"What a question!" I said. "You know, or rather you used to know, what my metaphysical 'position' is. . . . I believe I can see in nature the traces of an order, a plan—the reflection of divinity, if you like. . . . But the plan itself seems to me to be unintelligible to a human mind. . . . To answer you, then, I can fall back on no traditional doctrines. All I can honestly say is that I have never come across any visible sign of the survival of souls. . . . But to declare as a fact that the soul dies with the body strikes me as equally rash."

"You're very canny!" he said impatiently. "It is impossible that one of these hypotheses should not seem to you more probable than the other. . . . Do you live as if you believed or as if you did not believe in another life?"

"I certainly live as if I did not believe in a Day of Judgment; but that doesn't prove that I am sure of the non-immortality of the soul. It proves that I don't believe in the severity of a God who must at the same time be our Creator. . . . But if you give me a moment or two to think, I feel I can find arguments in favor of the hypothesis that the soul dies with the body. . . . Thought without body? It seems inconceivable. . . . Don't you think so? Our thinking is a tissue of images and sensations. . . . Sensations cease with the sentient organs, and the rebirth of images is bound up with the existence of a nervous system. . . . You know better than I do how certain physical deterioration of the brain cells causes an alteration, even a suppression, of personality. . . . It was you yourself who taught me that a man's thoughts can be transformed by the presence of spirochetes, the injection of certain glandular products. . . . All this shows a very strong link between the physical basis of our thinking and the thought itself. . . . And then, after all, there is syncope. . . . Do you remember, James, the day when my horse fell on me, in Flanders somewhere, and you found me unconscious in the meadow? I had been there for two hours, and I remembered nothing. . . . It did not look as if my soul had been living while my body was annihilated."

"That seems very poor reasoning to me," said the doctor, in a harsh, sarcastic voice. "I grant you that in your swoon you ceased for a period to be conscious of your personality. (Yet that is going a long way, for there are many patients who come round from a faint or an anaesthetic and remember extraordinary scenes, and sometimes describe the impressions of

a soul set free.) But that your personality was annihilated, the very fact of your awakening totally
disproves. . . . When you got up after your tumble
from your horse, you weren't a different man—you
were the same man. . . . If this experiment proves
anything, it would rather be that your personality
was able to survive when your body had seemingly
deserted it. . . . But we can imagine better. Nowadays, when a heart stops beating and lungs stop
breathing, we doctors say that the patient is dead.
. . . Very good. . . . But suppose that means were
found (and its not at all improbable that they may
be) for inducing a circulation of new blood in the
dead man's head. Will not the man live again?"

"I don't know. . . . It's possible."

"If he is reborn, will it be with the same or a different personality?"

"The same, of course."

"Then we're agreed. . . . But where will that
personality come from? Will you maintain that it is
suddenly formed, with all its vast landscape of
memories, with its passions and sentiments, in that
newly reborn body? Or is it the dead man's old soul?
And if the latter, are you not thereby granting that
it did *not* die with the body?"

"Why, James? If our memories are linked with a
definite structure of the brain, and if that structure
has not altered, the memories are reborn identical.
. . . To use a rough-and-ready image, but one that will
give you some notion of my thought, it is as if you

said, 'The ministry is empty all night, isn't it?' And yet when the clerks come back in the morning, they will busy themselves with the same matters. Therefore, the ministry has a personal soul which dwells there invisibly during the night?"

"An ingenious sophism!" said the doctor, as he poured out some wine. "But it has no substance. . . . For you're presupposing that the brain contains the outline of its images and memories just as the ministry contains its files. . . . Well, you must allow me my opinion as a doctor that we possess no proof at all of any such organization of the brain. The idea of cerebral localization is less and less favored by the specialists, and even were it true, it would not prove your assertion. . . . No, the more one studies the structure of the brain, the stronger is one's impression that it is, as your countryman Bergson says, a system of communication, a telephone exchange between the body and. something else. Naturally, if you destroy the exchange your communication ceases, but that doesn't prove that the interlocutor never existed, nor that he vanished with the instruments. . . ."

"Quite so, James. But in the case of the telephone exchange, I believe in the interlocutor because a simple experiment will enable me to trace him by proceeding to him in the flesh, on foot, on horseback, or by air. Who has ever traced this soul interlocutor of yours? Can you give me a single instance of thought without a corporeal basis?"

"Why certainly! You must see that if the body, the first cell, the first perceptible particle of protoplasm, were not preceded by a 'vital force,' a 'creative thought,' matter would never have·been organized into a living body . . . After all, it is rather surprising that you yourself should have formed a *body,* the body I see before me now, with carbon, oxygen, phosphorus, and a few other insentient elements. . . . And it's still more surprising that you thus constructed a man, rather than a bear or a shrimp. . . . Where was the material basis of the thought from which you were born? From what brain were transmitted the inherited thoughts and ancestral images that make you *you?"*

"Are you talking seriously, James? Don't you believe simply that this material basis was within the fertilized cell from which my body sprang? Biology is not my strong point, but. . . ."

"I can't help smiling!" he said. "Where have you seen any scientific proof, my dear fellow, that your body and mind were prefigured in a certain cell thirty-five years ago? You said just now, 'I believe in the interlocutor because a simple experiment will enable me to trace him.'. . . But in this case, what experiment have you made? What allows you to imagine that to enlarge a cell to a gigantic scale, beyond the power of any microscope, would enable you to discover in it the nose of your great-grandfather, or the puritanism of mine? And if you really believe so, do you think that such a belief is scientific?

That would be a great mistake. . . . That notion, if you have it, is a religion, neither more nor less proven than another, surprising only in a man who has just been declaring himself emancipated from any doctrine. . . . I know very well that the nineteenth century strained every nerve to reduce the spiritual to terms of the material. But it failed. Observation in no way proves that the mental, the sentimental, life is contained within the material life, but on the contrary, that the former supplements the latter with a whole unexplored domain. . . ."

The plump, pink headwaiter brought in our coffee. He looked pained. Guests at Johnson's, I dare say, did not usually argue heatedly on the immortality of the soul. I held my peace. James's arguments left me somewhat embarrassed. I offered him a cigarette, and for some time he smoked in silence.

"All the same," I said at last, "all the same. . . . Try the *reductio ad absurdum,* James. . . . Supposing that each single one of us has an immortal soul, where the deuce would the billions be who have lived? Where would the millions of billions go who have still to live? Where are the souls of brute beasts? If you were a theologian, you'd say they hadn't any. But you're a naturalist. Where are the souls of all the porpoises and kangaroos and crabs that ever existed? Don't you find such an idea inconceivable?"

"If I were a theologian, as you say, I should probably reply that those numbers which terrify you are as nothing in the sight of an all-powerful and infinite

God. . . . But you're talking now of an eternal survival of all personalities. I'm not asking so much as
that. Can't you imagine that every living body might
have attached to itself a certain quantity of a force,
the nature of which is unknown to us, but which, for
convenient reference, we may term the 'vital fluid'?
What's to prevent us from thinking that after death
this 'fluid' returns to a kind of common stock? Why
shouldn't there be a principle of the conservation of life, analogous to that of the conservation
of energy? Grant me that, and I shall say I'm satisfied."

"Satisfied? But my dear James, why do you attach
all this importance to such frail hypotheses?"

"That, my friend," he said, rising, "I shall explain
to you in an hour's time, if you will do me the favor
of coming back with me to the hospital."

IV

While we had been dining, a thick fog had come
down over the streets. The gleaming headlights of invisible cars planted it with rings of red and white
light. Ludgate Circus was a landscape of nightmare.
James bade me take his arm and guided me toward
a bus. He had not spoken a word since leaving the
hotel. When we were seated, I turned to him.

"What are we going to see?" I asked.

"Nothing perhaps. . . . You shall judge for yourself. . . . But in any case, you must realize that you're the first person to whom I am revealing my researches. . . . Besides, you'll understand. . . . But I'd rather not talk in here," he added, casting a hostile glance toward a lady in mourning who was sitting beside me.

The bus crossed the river in the midst of a veritable bank of yellow cotton wool. Factory fires on that baleful shore gleamed vast and pale through the flocculent gloom. The vibration of the bus made me drowsy.

"We get off here," said Dr. James abruptly.

We were in front of Saint Barnaby's. The lights of the hospital shone feebly in the enveloping cloud. With the sure movements of a man on his own ground, James led me across the quadrangles and under archways; and in a moment or two I recognized the iron door of the mortuary. For some time I had felt sure it was there that he was bringing me, and in spite of myself, I shuddered. My companion's nervous state seemed to be one of violent overexcitement. With what macabre exhibition did he propose to round off our evening? The door was shut and bolted, and James knocked once, then twice quickly.

"I'm here, doctor," came the insufferable voice of Gregory from inside.

I was annoyed with myself for my uneasiness, and could not overcome it. As a matter of fact, looking back on it in cool blood, I can now hardly find an explanation of its intensity. I had found this man Gregory distasteful, but I had no reason to think that he was anything but a harmless laboratory assistant. My acquaintance with James was of old standing, and nothing I knew of him could fail to fill me with confidence. True, he had greatly changed since the War, and I was not quite confident of his being in his right mind. But what could I have to fear? The sight of death? The years between 1914 and 1918 had accustomed me to that. Was I being made an unwilling accomplice? But an accomplice in what crime? I strained every nerve to make that effort at self-command which one made, ten years before, when a bombardment began; and I crossed the threshold, resolved on firmness.

"Good evening, doctor," said Gregory.

Then he noticed my presence. He looked surprised, and, I thought, rather put out.

"Hullo, you've brought someone along, doctor?" he said.

And taking James aside, he whispered a few words which I could not hear.

"It makes no difference," said James out loud. "My friend is a Frenchman, a total stranger to the hospital, and a loyal friend of mine throughout the War. He will hold his tongue."

"I hope so," said Gregory. "I certainly hope so. . . . We'd both lose our positions, doctor, if the gentleman did any talking."

"All right, all right—I tell you he won't,"

answered James impatiently. "Have you got the man?"

Stepping aside, Gregory opened the dissecting table to our view. I then saw that a body was lying on it, completely naked, with its head flung back; and I recognized the man with the ruddy-white beard I had seen that morning in his death agony. I had been wrong in taking him for an old man. Sickness had left marks of wear on his face, but the body was youthful, handsome, and muscular, and, in the pitiful limpness of death, left one with a cruel impression of wasted vigor. The left thigh was tattooed with a device of two entwined serpents, and the chest displayed a bark with swelling sails.

"We're late," said James. "This fog. . . . How long has he been there?"

"The last breath was about nine-forty, doctor. . . . And it's ten-thirty now."

"That's all right," said the doctor. "There's a chance yet. . . . Quick, Gregory, the weighing machine. . . ." And turning to me, he added, "Sit down on one of those benches. . . . Don't move; and not a word. . . . I'll explain later what you'll have seen. . . ."

Gregory had vanished under the tiers of seats. He returned bearing an apparatus which I identified, when he set it up, as a weighing machine with a dial and pointer on top, very much like those to be seen in railway stations. Its platform was large enough to support an outstretched human body. With James's help the assistant laid the corpse of the redheaded man on it, and fixed a small mirror at the tip of the pointer. Then, diving once more beneath the benches, he brought up a cylinder mounted on a fairly tall upright support. I heard a spring being turned. No doubt he was winding up some piece of clockwork mechanism.

"Make haste, Gregory, make haste!" said the doctor impatiently. "Are you ready? I'll put the lights out. . . ."

He turned a switch. All the lights in the amphitheater went out. And I then saw that a luminous ray, reflected by the mirror fixed to the point of the needle, struck the cylinder, which was slowly revolving. By this means, any movement of the pointer was matched by the much more extensive movement of a luminous point on the cylinder. It was the classic method which I had seen used long ago, in the physiology class, to augment the sensitiveness of a galvanometer.

I understood nothing of the experiment I was witnessing; but the scene had assumed a scientific, and therefore familiar, aspect, which reassured me. I was now alive to its curious beauty. The blackness, that feebly gleaming ray, that naked body vaguely outlined in the dark, James's face picked out for an instant by the ray—it all recalled those pictures of Rembrandt's wherein the philosopher, the alchemist, toils in the brown shadows relieved only by a yellow light from the narrow, unearthly windows.

For a few minutes the silence was complete, and then James's voice came out from the darkness.

"Are you beginning to grasp?" it said. "You gathered, of course, that the luminous spot on the cylinder indicates the weight of the body. . . . Well, now, look at the two phosphorescent marks showing the top and bottom of the cylinder. You see how the ray's point of impact is slowly dropping—the weight is diminishing. . . . The weight of a corpse always diminishes during the hours following death. . . . Why so? That's easy to understand: part of the moisture contained in the tissues is lost by slow evaporation, and there is no nutrition to replace it. . . . Observe that this drop is continuous, as you can see by noting that the luminous point falls steadily, and in fact there seems no reason why such evaporation should be anything but regular. . . . It is about an hour now since death took place. For half an hour more, within a few minutes, this phenomenon will continue without any change. After that you must watch the cylinder very closely."

There followed an extraordinary stillness. I could hear James and Gregory breathing. Slowly the luminous point kept sinking; and there this man lay, he who doubtless had once, to a wife and children, been the center of the world, now stretched on a metal platform, the object of an incomprehensible experiment. High up in the amphitheater the buzzer sounded—*tak-tak-tak . . . tak-tak. . . .*

"Twenty-five past one," said James, in a tone

which again made me aware of the extraordinary nervous tension he had shown earlier in the night.

I kept my eyes glued to the cylinder. I could distinctly hear the tick of a chronometer, which James no doubt was holding.

"One-thirty," he said.

A few seconds later I saw the spot of light drop sharply. The jump was very small, but easy to detect.

"Did you see, James?" I exclaimed.

"I've seen better things than that," said the sarcastic voice. "I didn't bring you here merely to observe *that* phenomenon."

And with that he turned on the lights again. Slightly dazzled, I saw once again Gregory's waxed mustache and the ruddy man lying there in one of those limp, clumsy positions assumed by corpses.

My calm had returned. I felt interested and curious; I had glimpses of what my friend was seeking. I felt passionately anxious to know his own interpretation of his experiment.

"Now you'll explain," I said.

"Wait," he answered me. "I must let Gregory get to bed. . . . Come up to my room and I'll let you see something else. . . . Thanks, Gregory. I'll be seeing you tomorrow."

"Shall I keep the heart for Professor Simpson tomorrow?" said the little man politely, taking the dead body in his arms to put it back on the dissecting table.

"Who cares about hearts?" said James with a

shrug. "Yes, of course; just do what they told you."
And taking my arm, he led me away.

V

"Well, James?" I asked, when he had settled me
in his solitary armchair, with a whisky on my right
and a cigarette box on my left.

"Well, my friend, I suppose you're expecting me
to explain this session to you. . . . But first I should
like to know what you yourself think of the things
you've just seen."

"I? Well, what am I to say? Our talk during dinner, and the experiment I've just witnessed, seem
to me to prove that you are in pursuit of—what shall
I say?—of the human soul. . . . And also that, be-
lieving in the spirit, you are seeking it by material
means. . . . Which, if you will excuse me, seems a
contradiction. . . . But I'm wrong to pass judgment,
as I don't even know what experiments you have
made apart from this evening's. So it is up to you to
talk and start off."

He was standing leaning against the mantelpiece.
He lit up his pipe. Behind the green curtain a gallop-
ing of sharp claws sounded along a wooden board.

"James, tell me the truth. Those *are* rats, aren't
they?"

" 'How now! A rat?' " he said with a smile. . . . "I
must take you to see *Hamlet* again. . . . There's a

new batch just now. . . . But we'll talk of rats all in good time. . . . Let's get back to men. . . . To begin with, I want to answer your first objection. You tell me that I'm seeking the spirit in the form of matter. But that's not quite right. . . . I am not seeking the spirit. I am seeking a certain form of energy which, when linked up with matter, will endow matter with that still unexplained property—life. . . . You will grant me, I think, that notwithstanding the claims of fanatical materialists, it has hitherto proved impossible to reproduce the reactions of living matter by any physical or chemical process. . . ."

"True. But there is a supposition that someday they will be explained. . . ."

"Oh, if you like!" he said impatiently. "One can suppose anything. . . . But there again, that is no longer science, but religion. . . . In any case, you will grant me that, scientifically or experimentally, I am entitled to say that we do not know what life is. . . . So there is no absurdity in seeking, as I am doing, the existence in living bodies of a form of energy different from all forms familiar to us. Observe, pray, that this search does not raise the problem of the soul in the religious or philosophic sense of the word; it transposes it, shifts it, sets it farther back. . . . Even if I succeeded in proving that in every living being there does exist a definite mass of 'vital fluid,' allowance would still have to be made, within that fluid itself, for spirit and matter; and then one would have to show how they are united. . . . I mention that in case any orthodoxy may make you distrustful a priori. . . ."

"My dear James," I said, "I have made my point of view in this connection quite clear, and I am listening in a critical but perfectly free spirit. . . . In any case, your idea of vital fluid is not a new one. Mesmer, who was one of the remoter causes of the French Revolution, had. . . ."

"I know, I know," said the doctor, pulling at his pipe. "What's more, he had a much more important successor, whom I dare say you know nothing about —the Baron von Reichenbach."

"You're right: I know nothing of him. Who was he?"

"He was an extraordinary character, put out of the way by the French police because he wanted to found a state. . . . A great chemist—it was he who discovered paraffin and creosote. . . . About 1860 he attacked the problem of the radiation of living bodies. He was the owner of several fairy-tale castles in Bavaria, some perched on mountains, others set beside lakes. And there he assembled subjects of peculiar sensitivity, people who could perceive in total darkness, around men and animals and flowers, a luminous fluid to which Reichenbach had given the name 'Od,' from a Sanscrit term meaning 'all-penetrating.' Reichenbach's subjects, in total darkness, saw emanations rising from bodies; they were neither smoke nor vapor, but resembled a sustained flickering. . . . A curious detail was that these emanations were reddish in color for the right side of the body, and bluish for the left. . . . As a matter of fact, I have tried to repeat Reichenbach's experiments. But I never found anything. When the three of us, you and Gregory and myself, were in total darkness just now, you didn't detect any 'odic flickering,' did you? And yet we were all in a state of extreme hyper-aesthesia at the time."

"No, I saw nothing."

"And around the corpse?"

"Nothing."

"Nor did I. And it has always been the same. . . . But I have found something else. . . . This is how it was. . . . I once read an account, in a medical paper during the War, of an experiment made by a certain Dr. Crooks. He described how he had weighed the corpses of animals, and had observed that, after a period approximately regular in a given species, there was an abrupt drop in weight. . . . In man, he reckoned this fall as averaging seventeen-hundredths of a milligram. From which he concluded that the soul does exist, and that it weighs seventeen-hundredths of a milligram. . . . In that crude form the communication was regarded as absurd. The said Crooks was put down as a madman, and nobody read his paper with care. . . . For my own part, his account struck me by its sincerity of tone and by its remarkable precision in details. . . . All the same, I would never have tried repeating these troublesome and unpleasant experiments if—" He broke off as if he regretted having started that sentence, and went on without concluding it. "Last year, as circumstances and hospital routine placed corpses at my disposal, it occurred to me to verify the facts registered by Crooks; and with some surprise I discovered that he had told the truth. . . . Only, he had stopped the experiment too soon. In man the normal curve of evaporation is almost always interrupted, not once, but three times by sudden falls. . . . The first, which you have observed tonight, takes place about one hour and thirty-five minutes after death, and is between fifteen- and nineteen-twentieths of a milligram; the second and third, which I did not wait for because I now know them all too certainly, follow the first at intervals of twenty minutes and one hour, respectively. . . . Were you going to say something?"

"Nothing important. . . . a mere comment. As you can never place your bodies on the scales except some minutes after death, you do not know, James, whether a phenomenon of the same category may not have taken place during those few minutes."

He reflected for a moment, and then said:

"Quite true. . . . But I come back to what I know. . . . Regarding the results of the experiment, no doubt is possible. . . . You have just seen them for yourself, everybody can verify them. . . . Let me add that I have repeated them with animals—whence the rats which intrigued you. And there, too, Crooks's results are correct. There is always a sharp drop, but its extent is very much less than in man. . . . In the case of a rat, it is so faint that it cannot be measured. . . . Such are the facts; the interpretation, of course, admits of argument. . . ."

His pipe had gone out. He relit it and looked at me. I was careful to say nothing. He continued.

"At this stage, this is what I put forward. It seems to me possible to suggest, not that the soul weighs seventeen-hundredths of a milligram, which would be oversimple; but that every living creature is animated (in your language you could almost say '*âme*') by a certain form of energy, still unknown, which leaves the body after death. That all energy possesses mass is something admitted by the post-Einstein physicists. You know that light can be weighed, and that theoretically light could be compressed in a receptacle. . . . Well, why not vital energy likewise? True, the weight of light is of a different order of size, something infinitely smaller than what we are observing here. But I don't see why that should be an argument against me. It merely proves that we are in the presence of a quite different phenomenon, which is not surprising. . . . States of matter are now known of such a kind that a ton of atoms reduced to their kernels could find room in my waistcoat pocket. . . . Do you follow me thus far, or do you think I'm quite crazy?"

"I find it very hard to accustom myself to these ideas, but your argument there is clear to me. . . . However, I will raise one objection. You apparently regard a human body as a living unity; but so far as we know, it is nothing of the kind. The different cells of the body don't all die at the same time. A heart lives longer than a brain. When I was in America I was shown in Carrel's laboratories how heart cells can be kept alive almost indefinitely by artificial means. I cannot remember the name of the scientist who once said that the cells of a body die like the inhabitants of a starving city—the weakest first. But if death is a series of stages, how is that idea to be linked with that of your sudden drops?"

"A very reasonable point; I had considered that myself. . . . The answer is, first, that I observe not one drop, but several; and then, that your idea of the individual death of cells is a hypothesis, but no more than a hypothesis. . . . If there does exist a certain force which may be the basis of what we call 'personality,' it is bound to disappear all at one time—doubtless at the instant of the heaviest fall; nevertheless, the personality of one of us is something quite distinct from the life of each of our cells. . . . A personality either exists, or does not exist. . . . Remember again, I have no wish to make the soul something material; but, as I explained just now, just as the soul is linked with the body for the expression of its thoughts and the perception of its sensations, so it is likewise possible that after quitting the body, it should be linked with this mysterious energy which we have just noted in the act of departure."

"You mean that personality could survive the

body, if the vital energy of that body could remain grouped in one single place?"

"Exactly. . . . But for the moment I make no affirmations. . . . I merely say it is not inconceivable."

"But in actual fact this energy does not remain grouped."

"We don't know at all, but, as I said when we were dining, just as the matter from which a body is made up returns under various forms to universal matter, so, at the moment of death, our vital force returns to some vast reservoir of spiritual energy until such time as, reunited to certain atoms of matter, it once more animates a living being."

"In other words, you believe in an immortality of the universal soul, but not in the survival of the individual?"

"You have the real French taste for ideas, *mon ami*. . . . At the moment you are drawing me into the field of hypothesis; and that has no bounds. . . . For my own part, the problem interesting me is much more restricted. . . . If one could gather up the vital energy of a human being, would one thereby have fixed his personality? Would that assure him, if not of immortality (all problems involving infinity surpass the human mind), at least of some measure of survival? That is what I am trying to find out."

"A little crazy, James—but interesting. . . . Well, what next? Have you tried to gather up this 'something' that weighs seventeen-hundredths of a milligram?"

"I have not yet found a means of trying it with a man. . . . I have tried it with animals. During the weighing-machine experiment, I have placed certain animals underneath glass bell jars—but what did I collect in them? Did they even collect anything? I have never been able to say. In the first place, I am obliged to lift the bell jar in order to withdraw the animal. Do its contents thereupon escape? I simply don't know. . . . Notwithstanding Reichenbach and his assertions, the vital fluid remains invisible; and that doesn't make observations easy. . . . Obviously experiments made with humans ought to give results more readily observed, as the quantities involved are greater. Three days ago I ordered a glass bell jar of a size large enough to cover the body of a man. I shall have it next week. . . . We'll see. . . . Are you likely to be still here?"

"I have to return to Paris for a few days, but my work is far from being completed, and I shall be back in London on Friday, about seven in the evening. . . . Will you dine with me then?"

"No, I can't leave the hospital on a Friday. . . . But come here yourself, and perhaps. . . ."

He looked at me long and steadily, like an architect gauging with his eye the strength of a beam or a wall.

"Of course," he said, "you'll stick to your promise not to breathe a word about what you've seen here. . . . It would mean the loss of my position and of the opportunity to continue my experiments. . . ."

I shook his hand, and left. I had great difficulty in finding my way back in the fog, and it was three o'clock in the morning before I got back to my hotel. I could not sleep.

VI

I am reaching the point in this story where circumstances led to my playing a larger part in it; and I must admit at once that, after my solemn promise given to James, I was blameworthy in talking to a French scientist, even indirectly, of his researches. But I had, I think, some excuse. In the first place, it was chance, and not my own intention, that during this period brought me into touch for the first time with Monestier. Further, as will be seen, the questions I asked him were such that he could not for a moment think that investigations of so strange a kind were really being carried out by a doctor. And finally, I am bound to say that the steps I took, rash though they may have been, enabled James to make great strides toward the solution of the problem.

I reached Paris on a Saturday, and dined that same evening with some friends. Taking my place at table, I found that I had Monestier as my neighbor. He had long been an object of my admiration, for he is not only, after Jean Perrin and Langevin, one of the greatest of physicists, but also a perfect writer. And I was charmed by the man himself, with his eyes as blue and lively as a child's, the soft clump of his white hair, and his swift, youthful voice. He talked first, I remember, about the works of Esnault-Pelterie and the possibility of a voyage to the moon.

"I shan't go, myself," he said. "My son will perhaps go. My grandson certainly. . . . In any case, there will be hundreds of volunteers."

"How will they breathe?" I asked.

"They will have oxygen with them," said Monestier. "And later, when a colony of human beings has been settled there, an oxygen market will be opened where the housewives will go every morning to get their supplies of breathable air. . . . The life will seem quite simple to those who live it. . . . What would Christopher Columbus have thought if the liner *Ile de France* had been described to him? Read your Jules Verne and Wells again. Almost all the dreams of the preceding generation have become the realities of today."

It was just then (and doubtless because he had sympathetically thrown the names of Jules Verne and Wells into the conversation) that a sudden and irresistible desire caught me to question him concerning the scientific value of Dr. James's investigations.

"I ought to tell you," I said to him, "that I am thinking of writing a fantastic story myself; and it is one on which, as I have the opportunity, I should be very glad to have a scientist's opinion. . . . Of course you'll think the subject quite absurd. . . . I know it is. But I'd like to know, supposing that a scientist was so foolish as to make certain experiments, what course he would take, what line of inquiry he would follow."

Whereupon I recounted to Monestier, as if it were a fictitious story, my conversations with James, and the experiments which I had winessed. He listened with good-humored amusement.

"It is not really so very absurd," he commented. "Why shouldn't there be 'psychons' as there are electrons? We know so little, after all. . . . Then what exactly do you want me to tell you? What experiments your doctor could make? Well, in his place I should first try to find out whether certain rays do not make visible this energy which he thinks he has collected in his flask. . . . Have you ever seen how certain fluorescent substances, invisible in broad daylight, become visible in darkness under ultraviolet rays?"

"No, never."

"I can show you that some time; it's a very pretty sight. . . . Could you come to my laboratory tomorrow?"

"I should be delighted."

And the next day I found him in a new building, surrounded by shining and complicated apparatus. When I entered, he was standing before a glass tube in which, on coming nearer, I could see rings of woolly light, mauve-pink in color, pale and unearthly.

"Ah, good day!" he said. "Look, here is a very odd phenomenon. . . . Look at this. . . . I pass a magnet right along the tube. . . ."

He was holding a small horseshoe of metal, and he shifted it slowly toward the right. Whereupon I saw the rings separate from each other, following the magnet and turning paler and more transparent. Then Monestier moved the magnet back toward the left; and the rings slipped into each other until they formed simply one small ring of a violet-colored substance.

"It is delightful!" I exclaimed. "But what is the explanation?"

"Ah," he said, "that is what I'm looking for! I don't yet know. . . . But you came along to see the phenomena of fluorescence. I mustn't waste your time."

In one corner of the room stood an extended apparatus, completely black, looking rather like a large-scale camera, covered with the cloth which photographers use when they are focusing.

"This is the apparatus that produces ultraviolet rays," said Monestier. "Visible light is shut off as it emerges by a black disk which lets only the invisible rays come through. . . . Look—will you kindly switch off the light. . . . The switch is farther to the left. . . . Good. Now I set the apparatus in action in the dark. . . . You see nothing. . . . If you put your hand over the path of the beam you will see it turn partly luminous, and if you leave it too long, you'll burn yourself. . . . Good. Now I place in front of the apparatus a flask filled with water. Naturally, it is invisible. . . . But I pour a fluorescent substance into the water and—look!"

Suddenly two spots of steely blue appeared in the darkness, like planets hanging in the night. They spread out, curling in slow spirals, growing larger and fainter, nebulae becoming more and more attenuated. A liquid smoke filled the whole flask with an unreal, luminous cloud.

"How beautiful!" I said. "It is like being present at the creation of matter. . . . But why isn't all that visible in ordinary light?"

"My dear sir," said Monestier with a smile, "the 'becauses' of science are nearly always statements of observed fact. . . . You remember Molière's *'Quia est in eo virtus dormitiva.'* . . . Because there are fluorescent substances which are visible in ultraviolet rays. . . . But to revert to your story—and I dreamed a lot about it in the night—nothing prevents one from supposing that your 'vital fluid' is fluorescent. . . . The doctor in your tale could certainly borrow an apparatus in his hospital similar to this one. . . . Let him place one of his bell jars in the path of the rays and—who knows?—perhaps he will see the 'psychons' suddenly become luminous."

"Yes—a very good idea. . . . And do you think that the glass of the domes would not allow the energy which they contain to escape? Wouldn't he need metal ones? Or rock crystal?"

"Ah, that I don't know. . . . It all depends on the nature of your fluid, which is unknown to me. But I see no a priori reason why glass should be inadequate. . . . If it is, you can suppose that your hero tries a colloidal glass. Then you'll have beautiful red flasks in your story. . . . But I'll show you something else."

He showed me blades of soap, infinitely thin, in which there were formed disks of vivid, changing colors, and I did not venture to say more to him about "my story."

VII

I returned to London on the Friday evening. A bad crossing left me too tired to go out again the same night, and it was not until the Saturday morning that I went to see James at the hospital. He was not in his room, but the door was open and I went inside to wait for him. The great curtain was pulled back. The shelves which this curtain had hidden on my first visit held a small pair of scales, an inverted glass bowl, a few small bottles. While awaiting my friend's return, I looked at the women's photographs which stood along the mantelpiece and on the writing table, and I then saw (what I had not observed on the first day) that they were all portraits of the same woman, a girl, indeed, almost a child. The expression of the face was gentle and ingenuous, with charming features, and hair so very fair as to seem almost white. In nearly all these portraits the young woman wore costumes of bygone times. Was she an actress? Did she like to set off her beauty with different adornments? I was lost in that musing into which the enigma of a lovely face always plunges us, when I heard footsteps. I turned around. James was behind me. He laid a hand on my shoulder, and himself glanced at the portraits for a moment.

"Well!" he said at last in his hoarse voice. "You've got back, have you? And how did you find 'the Gay City'?"

"Very pleasant. . . . I don't know any city more charming than Paris in springtime. . . . But that's not the question. I believe, James, that I picked up some valuable suggestion over there for your researches."

"For my researches? How so?"

I told him of my indiscretion, making it plain that it could entail no dangers to himself. I described what I had seen in Monestier's laboratory, and gave him as clear an account as I could of what the scientist had told me.

"Do you understand, James? It seems to me that if you could pass a beam of ultraviolet rays above the body just when you think something escapes from it, you would perhaps be able to see the fluid become luminous. . . . Of course, it may just as well be the contrary—but couldn't you try? This hospital surely has an ultraviolet-ray apparatus?"

"Oh, yes," he said, musing. "The only difficulty would be to get it in the dissecting room. . . . But that shouldn't be really impossible. . . . Yes, thanks very much—it's a good idea. . . . I have often seen experiments in fluorescence; but I hadn't thought of applying them here. In any case. I can make a test in my own room on one of the small animals. Will you come over tomorrow night? We'll do this together."

I promised to come, but I asked him, if he had to kill a rat or any other creature, to do so before my arrival, as I greatly disliked such a sight. He laughed at me a little, and told me that the animals would not suffer, as he anaesthetized them beforehand with an injection.

* * *

The state of excitement in which I found James next evening is past imagining. The sound of my step on the staircase brought him out of his room, and when I reached the landing he held out both hands to me.

"Look here, old man," he said in a low voice, "we've got a solution, thanks to you."

"What do you mean?"

"Come in and have a look."

The room was dark, but James guided me from behind with a hand on each of my shoulders.

"Be careful," he said. "The apparatus is in the middle of the room. . . . Keep a little to your left. . . .

Farther. . . . Right. . . . Now straight in front of you. . . . Do you see anything?"

Over toward the fireplace I could discern a faint glow, about the size of a nut, but more elongated. Going closer, I saw that the interior of this luminous kernel contained darker currents revolving extremely slowly. The whole thing reminded one of the appearance of certain photographs of celestial nebulae.

"What have you got there?" I asked him. "It's curious, and rather beautiful in a way. . . ."

"I'll let you see it in the light," he said.

He moved away for a moment. The light in the middle of the room went on. I saw on the mantelpiece a small glass bell jar, beneath which lay a dead rat stretched on its side. The warm glow had vanished. I looked at James inquiringly.

"You look very surprised," he said. "But I have applied the idea you gave me. . . . What you saw just now was a small mass of—I dare not call it matter—let's say, if you like, of the luminous fluid which appeared under the beam of the ultraviolet rays at the top of the jar, twenty-one minutes after the animal's death."

I was overwhelmed, scarcely able to believe what I had just seen and heard.

"But this is extraordinary, James. . . . Nobody has ever thought of this. . . . It is a great discovery— don't you think so? And where is it now, your fluid? I don't see anything in the globe."

"Quite true. Nothing is visible in ordinary light,

and that explains why neither I nor anybody else ever noted the phenomenon before. . . . But your method, or that of your physicist friend if you like, is the right one."

"I'd like to see it again."

He switched off the light and turned on the apparatus. Instantly the tiny elongated kernel shone out with its soft nebular gleam.

"Really, James, I'm beginning to think that you are on the path of a wonderful and unforseeable future. . . . Do you think that the personality—no, one can't talk of the personality of a rat—do you think that the individuality of this creature persists in some form allied to this little glow?"

"I know no more than you do, old man. . . . All I can say is that it seems to me possible, even probable . . . and also, that I've decided to repeat the experiment on a man as soon as I have a larger bell jar. . . . And further, note that this fluid, luckily for us, is lighter than air and collects at the top, a fact which makes it quite easy to preserve even if the bowl has to be lifted to withdraw the body."

We stood silent for a moment or two in the darkness, gazing at this light which was perhaps the manifestation of a mysterious presence. At last James turned on the light again.

"How surprising it is," I said, "that such important and simple facts should hitherto have eluded mankind!"

"Why?" said James. "Isn't it the history of all

scientific phenomena? The data of all the great discoveries have existed in nature for thousands of years. What was lacking was a mind to interpret them. When the cave dweller dropped a stone into the stream beside his rocks he could have discovered, as Galileo did later, the laws of the velocity of falling bodies. . . . He didn't think about it. . . . Ever since the earth has been the earth, thunderstorms have provided wonderful experiments which could have shown all mankind the existence of electricity. . . . They were explained by the wrath of Jove. . . . Men have always been surrounded, and the atmosphere has always been traversed, by the rays of which our modern physicists make use; yet these rays remained invisible and elusive, like the vital force of my rat."

"Poor beast! Take it away, James. . . . I hate seeing that corpse among the photographs of that lovely woman there. . . ."

And after a moment's hesitation I added:

"Who is she?"

"Don't you know her?" said James. "That is Edith Philipps. The young actress, you know. . . . The whole of London is crowding to see her play Ophelia just now. . . . Haven't you been? I must take you one of these evenings."

"Take away the rat, James."

Carefully he raised the globe, and drawing the animal out by its long tail, he wrapped it up in a piece of paper.

"Now," he said, "we must see if our light is still there."

He repeated the experiment. The little ball of light was gleaming at the top of the jar.

VIII

My visits to Saint Barnaby's Hospital became of almost daily occurrence. I continued my work at the British Museum because I was forced to, and because I could not spend the daytime with Dr. James, whose profession left him little freedom; but my friend's researches were of greater interest to me than my own. Every day I waited impatiently the hour he had appointed for me. In the reading room itself, instead of working, I kept watching my neighbors, a girl with tortoise-shell spectacles, a little Hindu with curly hair, and imagined them lying on Gregory's grim balance. And when the hour came around, I hastened over to the city of chimneys and wharves.

Twice a week, on Wednesdays and Saturdays, the thoroughfare leading to the hospital was occupied by the humble street market which I had noticed on the occasion of my first visit. I enjoyed stopping beside the open-air booths where they sold fish, and books at a penny apiece, and old boots. Sometimes I had a talk with the hawkers. One of them, Mr. William Slutter, was a favorite of mine, on account of his astonishing natural distinction and his handsome head, which was like that of an aged aristocrat. He sold for sixpence queer little cigarette lighters on which a pig, with uplifted trotter, made the spark fly. "Wonderful joke!" he kept calling. "They never let you down. . . . I was sold out yesterday. I've only a few left." As a matter of fact I never saw him sell a single one. But he kept his good-mannered smile and an air of confidence in life. Nothing was further from my thoughts when I was talking with him one Wednesday about the difficulties of his trade than that he would be the subject during the very next week of the most extraordinary of experiments.

Yet so it turned out. Mr. William Slutter contracted a virulent pleurisy and was brought to Saint Barnaby's in a state that left no hope. That same day one of the big stores which prided itself on being able to supply anything, delivered to Dr. James the bell jar large enough to cover a human body, as he had ordered three weeks before. That evening, when I accompanied James on his round of the ward, I was taken aback at finding William Slutter's usually peaceful features there, ablaze with fever. "Wonderful joke. . . ." he kept calling. "Only a few left. . . ." And the next night, at midnight, I saw him again in the dissecting room.

I was beginning to be inured to this macabre spectacle. James, on the contrary, was in great agitation that night. He had helped Gregory to hide the gigantic globe beneath the rising tiers of seats, and was afraid lest the little man might break it as he

lifted it with our help on to the table and set it over
the corpse. The doctor had had to give up the idea
of using the weighing machine, as it would have
been difficult, if not impossible, to keep the globe
balanced on the platform. On the other hand, he
had again obtained the loan of the ultraviolet-ray
apparatus. Gregory was not aware of the nature of
our new researches; he no longer understood what
the doctor was doing, and gave us only clumsy and
ill-humored help.

At last poor William Slutter lay outstretched
under the huge jar, and the contrivance was placed
so that its top should come into the line of the rays.
These manipulations took so long that we had only
six minutes left until the moment when, according
to the now familiar timetable of these experiments,
"something" was sure to happen. James had his eye
on the clock and told Gregory to put the lights out.
I watched the invisible top of the globe, trying hard
not to lose its position. The waiting seemed endless.

"One minute," said James.

I began to count slowly. One . . . two . . . three . . .
four. . . . And I had reached fifty when I saw a faint
blue mist appearing. At first it seemed shapeless and
as if diffused over the whole width of the beam. But
this stage was so brief that I could not observe it.
Immediately the vapor became condensed in a milky
mass, about four inches long, the base of which was
horizontal, with its rounded top following the curve
of the globe. This mass was neither motionless nor

homogeneous. Currents of lighter and darker color were visible in it. I cannot describe it better than by asking you to imagine the smoke of several cigarettes, of varying density and slightly different colors, super-imposing their rings and spirals until they formed an object of well-defined outline.

"Doctor!" came the startled voice of Gregory. "Doctor! Doctor! Do you see that ball of light?"

"Keep quiet!" said James's grating voice.

I saw the doctor's head come into the field of the rays from the apparatus, and some of his features were for an instant lit up. Then he vanished into the darkness again. I could feel, though I could not see, that he was leaning, to watch it more closely, over the strange substance which he made his prisoner. I thought of William Slutter. . . . Did there really remain, under that glass bell, some fragment of what once had been that simple and contented soul? Was it possible that everything which had given life to that inanimate body was not concentrated in that tiny space? Were we holding there some impersonal force, or were we holding the individual William Slutter? Could he see us? Was he conscious of his incredible adventure? Was he thinking at that mo-ment—"Wonderful joke. . . ."? And if the least chance of his consciousness existed, had we any right to keep a soul captive?

"Lights, Gregory," said James's voice.

I was surprised to see again the doctor, the little assistant with his waxed mustache, the apparatus with its black cloth cover, and there, under that inverted bowl now deprived of its gleam, the corpse of an old man with a white mustache.

* * *

James looked at me with a nod of his head. I felt that he himself was overwhelmed by the success.

"You saw that ball of light, sir?" Gregory asked me.

"We all saw it," said James in an impatient tone. "What I now want, Gregory, is for you to keep this bell jar for me without breaking it, and especially *without turning it up.* . . . Do you understand?"

"Yes, Doctor," he replied humorously. "But don't give me another of these, for I shouldn't know where to stow it. As it is, if the students were to find it. . . ."

"I said nothing about another one," said James. "We'll give you a hand to carry this one underneath the seats."

And the three of us carried out this maneuver, not without difficulty, and then left Gregory. The little man seemed taciturn. When we were out in the hospital quadrangle under the starry sky, I said to James:

"I think you ought to give him some explanation. . . . You need him. . . . Now this evening. . . ."

"You're wonderful, my boy! What do you expect me to tell him? He knows as much as you and I do. . . . Can you yourself explain what we have seen?"

I told him that I could do no such thing, but that the experiment seemed to confirm all the theories he had put forward to me on the evening of our first dinner. If his hope had been to catch and preserve something of human beings after their death, he was on the track of such a possibility. I further admitted that I did not see what this success was leading to, for even admitting that he had the soul of poor William Slutter under his globe, he could not enter into communication with it. And I added that I was doubtful regarding his right to keep this unknown substance in captivity.

"For after all, James, suppose that the law of human nature really is that a vital fluid escapes from our body after death, to merge with some universal reservoir of life, why and how should we stand in its way? Your globes are not eternal, and a day will come when, despite you, William Slutter will cease to be William Slutter. And what will you then have done but vainly prolonged an existence, under conditions which perhaps are dreadful? You have made an amazing discovery, and one which will give you one kind of fame when you choose to make it public. . . . But you must confine the risk in these experiments to the bounds of strict necessity. 'There are more things in heaven and earth, Horatio. . . .' "

"That reminds me," he said, "that I must take you to see *Hamlet* one evening. . . . Good night!"

I could hardly have visited Saint Barnaby's Hospital so often without making the acquaintance of some of the medical staff. On several occasions James had taken me to a meal in the dining room of the resident members, where I had had some conversation with my neighbors, and I became particularly friendly with Dr. Digby, a mental specialist of the staff. I have always had a strong inclination, which I cannot explain very readily, toward the society of medical psychologists. . . . Experience of abnormal persons seems to give them a keener and more ingenious understanding of the normal. To myself, striving to be a writer and to understand mankind, their conversation always provided valuable lessons. Besides, I found Digby unusually congenial. He was a short bald man, with a look of wisdom in his eyes, who spoke in a very soft voice, with precision and intelligence.

On the day following the evening I have just described, I arrived in advance of the time fixed by James, and was strolling in the grounds of Saint Barnaby's, on the flowered terrace bordering the river, when I met Digby in a long white coat.

"Hullo," he said, "are you alone? Our friend isn't ill, is he? I didn't see him at lunch."

"I think he is all right, Dr. Digby, but he won't be free for a quarter of an hour."

He began to say something, stopped hesitantly, and then went on.

"Oh! Then this is just—No. . . . Yes. . . . As you have a quarter of an hour to spare, come into my room."

It was a very well-lit room, right on the terrace itself, and furnished with countless files and card-index cases.

"Cigarette? Whisky?" asked Digby. "No? Well now, listen. . . . As I've got the chance of seeing you alone for a moment, I'd like to talk to you about James. You're a friend of his; you're a stranger to the hospital; you can perhaps do us a great service."

"I should very much like to, if it is possible. But in what way?"

"I shall tell you. . . . But first of all it must be understood anything I say to you is confidential and cannot be repeated by you to anyone, even to himself. . . . That's understood, isn't it?"

"Of course."

"Good. . . . Well, I have reason to think that you are in the know about certain mysterious experiments which James is said to be carrying on, to some quite incomprehensible end, and in which he makes use of the corpses of patients dying in this hospital. Am I right?"

"What an examination! I cannot answer, doctor. . . . And I must ask you not to take that reply either as an affirmative or a denial. . . . It merely indicates that I regard my friend's action as depending solely on his own conscience."

"I quite approve your attitude," said Digby with a smile. "But from my point of view I am convinced that I am doing my duty when I tell you that the hospital authorities have been startled. . . . So far no inquiry has been ordered, mainly because everybody here is well disposed toward James, and also because the experiments as described seem absurd, though harmless."

"It seems to me in fact," I said, "that if one can dissect a dead body, one can all the more——"

"Be careful!" he said. "You're going to say more than you wish. . . . Understand me. . . . If these rumors get round beyond medical men to those less tolerant persons, the board of management, our friend might well find himself in rather serious trouble. But that is my least important motive. I am chiefly afraid of— 'Oh,' you'll think, 'these specialists see their pet subject everywhere!' But never mind!—I am chiefly afraid that certain researchers might prove a danger to James's mental welfare; and it is about his state of mind, if you will allow me, that I should like to have a word with you, because, I repeat, the circumstances seem to enable you to be of service to him yourself. . . . To begin with, do you know anything of his personal history?"

"What do you mean by his 'personal history'? I got to know him during the War. Of what may have happened to him before then I know nothing. Nor indeed of his sentimental history since the War, for he is like all you English, not a man to talk much about these things."

"Well, I must tell you what I think it necessary for you to know. . . . In March, 1914, James married a young Danish girl of great beauty, who was studying medicine in London. I knew her quite well. She was a woman of surprising intelligence; candid, too, and generous, but in no way suited to English life; but she had never loved James. On the other hand, he worshiped her, and I believe that she must have married him out of pity for the violence of the feeling she inspired in him. . . . When James went out to France at the end of 1915, Hilda James felt herself completely stranded here and returned to her own country. There she met a young man more suited to her taste. She wrote to James telling him so, loyally but without trying to soften the blow. . . . She asked for her freedom. He rebelled, and refused. . . . One day, at the front, he learned that she had died in some obscure, dramatic circumstances, about which I know little. . . . He has never got over it."

"How mysterious people are, doctor! So when I was living in the same Flanders dugout with James, he had just gone through this drama—and I never knew it!"

"Yes. . . . That impotence of self-expression is at once the strength and the danger of our national character. . . . We keep ourselves to ourselves. . . . We 'repress,' as the layman now says with rather naïve pedantry. . . . It is not without dignity, but it is a dangerous thing for one's mental balance. . . . In James's case, which I have followed at pretty close quarters, I was genuinely alarmed during the first few years after the War ended. . . . He lived then in a solitude, a sentimental starvation, which a Frenchman like yourself, I suppose, could hardly imagine. . . . Had it not been for his work at the hospital, in which fortunately he was interested, I doubt whether his reason would have stood the strain. . . . Then, finally, when he was spending a holiday with his people in Wiltshire, he received an urgent call, in the absence of the local doctor, to see a young girl who was taken ill. She was an actress."

"Miss Edith Philipps?" I said.

"Ah! So he's spoken of Miss Philipps, has he?"

"No . . . at least, only just. . . . But I saw her photograph in James's room and asked who she was."

"So you know that she is very beautiful. But you haven't been in a position to observe, as I have, her close resemblance to the girl who was once James's wife. . . . That was certainly the reason why he became attached to her from the first day he set eyes on her, and with an intensity that has been constantly growing. . . . Do not imagine that she is his mistress. She is unmarried and lives with her father, Gerald Philipps, who was himself one of our leading actors. She would certainly be married were it not for her health, which is so frail that we medical men can hardly tell how she can possibly withstand the strain of her calling. . . . What does she think of our friend? Does she love him? Does she feel affection, or indifference, toward him? I have never seen them together, and all I know of them comes to me from third parties. I know only that he is desperately attached to her, that he spends all his free time with her, and that he knows her to be seriously ill and lives in terror of losing her. . . . That is what I wanted to tell you so as to help you a little in your relations with him. . . . I don't want to add any of the conclusions which I myself draw from these given facts, because you are too intimate with him, and I know from experience, alas, how dangerous it is to plant suggestions in a hypersensitive soil where they immediately become sources of infection. . . . Excuse my frankness!"

"I am grateful to you, Dr. Digby. But I don't altogether understand. . . . What do you want me to do? I have no authority over James; I do not know Miss Philipps; and besides, I shan't be staying much longer in England—even if I wanted to, I couldn't. When I leave, I shall probably lose sight of James."

"That is all quite true, and I am asking nothing definite of you. . . . I merely wished you to know the facts, so as not to find yourself walking blindfold on difficult ground. . . . Now it is for yourself to judge. . . . If you can bring our friend within a reasonable interval to forsake this dangerously heretical quest of his, I think you will have rendered him a service, and even a twofold service. . . . But go along and see him quickly, for I've kept you more than your quarter of an hour."

I left him. When I reached James's room, the buzzer was ringing its two-four, two-four summons. . . . James had been called down to a ward and I had to wait for him. And I then observed that one among the photographs on the mantelpiece, the largest, was that of a different woman. I had noticed it the first time, because its resemblance to the other woman whose portraits surrounded it was truly astonishing.

X

I had not paid much heed to James's proposal, a few days earlier, to go and see *Hamlet*. The days and nights I was then spending with him, among his patients and sharing in his researches, seemed to me as beautiful and as varied as the greatest dramas. But after my talk with Digby I was naturally fired with a desire to meet Edith Philipps, and I reminded James of his promise. He told me he would ask for seats on his first free evening.

On the way to the theater he explained that the company was that of a theater in a working-class district. The critics had been so enthusiastic in their praise of the young man who played Hamlet, and of an unknown actor's Polonius, and above all of the Ophelia of Miss Philipps, that a West End manager had provided a theater for the players. Whereupon the whole of London had been rushing to see them, Shakespeare became the fashion, and many people came out declaring that they had just seen *Hamlet* for the first time. This, said James, was certainly true of the majority, but England discovered *Hamlet* in this way every fifty years. His friend's father, Gerald Philipps, had himself made his name half a century ago in the title part, and had "revealed" this unknown author, William Shakespeare, to the English of 1875.

To myself, as to the spectators at whom James had smiled, *Hamlet* was a new play that evening. These actors had shown a simple, but all too rare, discretion in playing Shakespeare's text without cuts. The young man who took the part of the Prince of Denmark played with vigor and straightforwardness. When he spoke the lines—

> "How weary, stale, flat and unprofitable
> Seem to me all the uses of the world. . . ."

he seemed as closely akin to our French selves as the youthful Barrès or Benjamin Constant. It was the young man of all time. And so too with Miss Philipps: from her first entrance I could see that she was the young girl of all time. In her opening scene with Polonius she displayed a blend of the demure, the artlessly forward, the childishly submissive, which I found enchanting.

"James," I said to him in the interval, "your friend is adorable!"

He seemed happy.

"You can tell her yourself shortly," he said. "I have told her that we would have supper together. . . . Are you pleased?"

"Delighted! It is excellent. . . . I've only one criticism—the Ghost. The Ghost disappointed me. Why make him speak from the wings? It is beneath the swords that Shakespeare's 'old mole' should cry his 'Swear! Swear!' Do you remember Goethe's comment on that point in *Wilhelm Meister?* Goethe thinks that the Ghost ought to disappear underground, and that a tongue of flame should spring from the ground to show where he is."

"The odic flickering?" said James, glancing at me with the faintest of smiles. . . . "I wonder what the ghost of William Slutter is doing at the moment?"

"I wonder indeed! Is he still in the bell jar?"

"Yes, I saw him still there last night; the glass prison is keeping him for us faithfully."

"Don't you want to restore him to liberty, James?"

He laid a finger on his lips. In front of us stood an attendant offering ices and boxes of chocolates. The bell announced the end of the interval. We were plunged once more into the world of Shakespeare.

It will no doubt seem surprising to find me speaking in such detail of a performance of *Hamlet* in the middle of a narrative so different in its subject. But I have two sound reasons for that. First, this was the evening when I made the acquaintance of Miss Philipps, who, as you will see, plays an important part in the secret which I wish to reveal in these pages. And further, I know not why, the atmosphere of *Hamlet* remains linked for me with the memory of Dr. James. It was the only occasion on which I could gauge the depth of hidden, desperate feeling which lay beneath the tragic but impassive mask. At the moment in the players' scene when Hamlet feels the shame of his own calmness in contrast with the actor's feigned emotion—

> . . . all his visage wan'd;
> Tears in his eyes, distraction in 's
>   aspect. . . .
> . . . What would he do,
> Had he the motive and the cue for
>   passion
> That I have?

—I saw James lean forward and open his lips as if he were on the point of crying these lines aloud himself. During the scene of Ophelia's madness, for the first and only time in my experience of him, I saw a tear slip down his cheek. And there Edith Philipps, it must be said, was deeply moving. Her eyes looked forth upon a transparent world. Her voice came singing and speaking in a monotone, with infinite softness, and she held out invisible flowers. "There's rosemary, that's for remembrance; pray, love, remember. . . ." She turned my thoughts also to so many things past and beautiful.

"Do you know," James said to me in the interval, "what is the most admirable thing in her playing? It is this—she succeeds in giving the impression, which madwomen in real life will often give, that madness is an almost conscious refuge. . . . Ophelia no longer wishes to see this horrible world; she has created another, the world of flowers, and her memories, and she will go on talking of it in her soft, implacable voice, to the very end. . . . Really, there is nothing in the theater more deeply human than that!"

When the stage had been strewn with corpses, and the young Fortinbras had had the Prince borne off upon the shoulders of four captains, and the audience had applauded loud and long, and the orchestra had played *God Save the King,* we came out in silence.

"What a crowd of corpses!" I said at last.

"As in life," said James. "Will you come round the theater with me to meet Edith at the other door? She must be ready by now, for she has had time to change during the last act."

We found her ready, as he had said, and waiting for us with the stage-door keeper. She was a thoroughly simple young girl, ingenuously pleased by the few compliments I paid her, as if she had not already been told by every critic in London that she was an actress of genius. James took us to a little French restaurant. There, in the light, I could see Miss Philipps better. She was every bit as beautiful as her portraits, but startlingly pale. During supper she was very gay. I was a little disappointed by the quality of her remarks; but isn't one always disappointed in an actress whom one has just seen in a masterpiece? Unconsciously one has endowed her with the spirit of Shakespeare or Musset; one has wished, almost hoped, that she may prove in actual life to be Juliet, or Desdemona, or Camille. And one finds—a child. It calls for a gift of greater penetration than I then possessed to detect in her the poetry she really held. I can now see the traits in Edith Philipps that made her wonderfully Shakespearean. James himself had realized them long before. I was touched by the tender admiration he showed toward her. And we parted on coming out of the restaurant, as he wished to take her home to her father's before he returned to the hospital.

XI

If I have succeeded in conveying any idea of James's character, you will have realized by now that when we met again, nothing further was said by either of us about Edith Philipps. I made several attempts to "start him off" on the subject, by taking up one of the photographs on the mantelpiece and looking at it with close attention. But I never succeeded. I regretted this, not only from curiosity, but because I believed (as I still believe) that my friend's unhappiness would have been lessened if he could have given utterance to the deep, bewildering passions which gripped him.

I had also tried several times, in accordance with my promise to Dr. Digby, to divert him from his researches. I pointed out to him that Gregory was now freeing himself from his influence, that the little man now only gave his help distrustfully and grudgingly, and that even the banknotes which James gave him more and more freely hardly brought forth a single word of thanks. The doctor likewise had observed these disturbing symptoms; but he did not make his visits to the dissecting room any less frequent. It must be admitted that his investigations had taken a very curious turn, and that I myself, though disapproving them, could not but follow them with intense interest.

In the first place, James had been struck with the difficulties involved in the handling and safeguarding of these huge glass bell jars, and had conceived the simple but ingenious notion of having them fitted at the top with a small globe, about four inches in diameter, communicating with the large one by a glass tube. Observing events under the ultraviolet rays, we saw, as might be expected, that the fluid rose from the larger vessel into the small one. The latter then became almost entirely luminous, the bell jar itself remaining dark. It was a simple matter to cut the connecting tube with a blowpipe and seal it, and so to preserve the "matter" or "energy" which was our concern, in a much reduced volume. By welding a new tube surmounted by a small globe to the same bell jar, the latter could continue to be used so long as it was not broken by careless handling.

These small globes, which could be easily carried

about, had been preserved by the doctor in his own room. To avoid confusion he had gummed on each a small label showing the name of the person from whom the contents had been obtained, and the date of the event which everybody else would have called their "death," but which James called their "metamorphosis." Globe No. 1 was that of William Slutter; No. 2 was an old eel seller, Mrs. Prim; No. 3 was a Norwegian seaman. There were by now seven in all, set side by side on an empty shelf in James's room. I spent hours contemplating them. They looked like soap bubbles suddenly and miraculously solidified. Inside each there stretched shifting strands of mingling blue and green, which, one convex, the other concave, followed the curve of the ball. It was merely, I think, the reflected image of window, sky, and trees in the two surfaces of the sphere. But sometimes I fancied I could see other and stranger shapes quivering within.

"Ah," the doctor would say, when he found me in contemplation before the shelf, "you're having a look at my 'souls,' are you?"

"How I wish you would set them free, James!"

"Later on," he would say, "later on. . . . When I've found out all I can learn from them."

From time to time he made an examination with the rays, to be sure that his "souls," or rather, as he used to say, his "fluid ghosts," had not escaped through the transparent walls of their prison. He observed no change. Every time he found that same

milky gleam, the same stirring of whirling shapes. An incomprehensible, but real, life was maintaining itself inside the globes.

James had discovered that the fluid exerted a distinct action upon certain external objects. If one brought a screen of fluorescent substance close to one of the globes, it was faintly lit up. For a long time I hoped that it might thus prove possible to enter into communication with the "ghosts." The luminosity of the screens subjected to the action of the globes continually varied; and by long or short periods of light a conversation might have been practicable. But all my efforts at interpreting these signs were in vain. James, for his part, tried to "bombard" the psychons, a first time with the help of X rays, and a second time by making use of radioactive elements. These last experiments, besides yielding no results, were distasteful to me. I regarded them as at once useless and cruel. The word "cruel" may seem surprising—but what did we know of the effect of these atomic bombardments on a substance which might well be sentient? I had argued this matter quite frequently with James; and over the question of a much simpler experiment, yet one which seemed to me much more blameworthy, our arguments were resumed, but so fiercely this time that for a moment I almost thought they would put an end to our friendship.

I had been away for a couple of days, engaged in some library researches at Oxford. Visiting my friend on my return, I found him examining two globes added to his collection during my absence, bearing the numbers 8 and 9. No. 8, he told me, was Agatha Lind, a young dancer who had committed suicide with veronal; No. 9 a Russian, Dimitri Roskoff, who had died of cancer. I was surprised to observe that instead of cutting the tube, and so making the globes perfectly spherical, James had in each case left the tube on the globe, contenting himself with sealing the extremity.

"Hullo, have you adopted a new method, James?" I asked. "I don't like it. . . . You rob our soap bubbles of all their beauty."

"You don't know what I want to do," he answered. "I have my reasons—you'll see. . . . I even think you will be pleased with me, you who are always complaining of possible cruelty in leaving a soul 'imprisoned in solitude.' "

"What do you mean?"

"It's quite simple. . . . Suppose that I place these two tubes in communication, one of the two globes being upside down above the other, what will happen?"

"I don't know. . . . Probably the two fluids will mingle and fill the whole space."

"Just what seems likely to me, too. . . . But then you will no longer have one solitary soul; you will have two souls joined in a closer, more intimate way than is conceivable in any earthly union. . . . What's wrong? Don't you think that's so?"

"I don't know at all, James, but it seems to me a

monstrous idea, and I cannot understand your conceiving it. . . . What! You would go and choose two beings at random who don't know each other, who would perhaps loathe each other, and you would force them, as you say, into a kind of union more intimate than any other, one that you yourself cannot even imagine? And you would do this for no reason, just from curiosity? No, not even from curiosity—because what will you ever know about the result of your attempt? Nothing—because, even granting that we are here in the presence of sentient and conscious beings, you are powerless to enter into communication with them!"

James looked at me solemnly, and even sadly.

"How unfair and passionate you are!" he said. "You know I am not a wicked man. . . . Very much the contrary. . . . I've had too many sorrows to be wicked. . . . I can understand other people condemning my researches, but you. . . . You ought to have realized long ago that I wouldn't occupy myself with these matters if I had not hopes of their possibly opening up great hopes, infinite vistas, for others. . . . Have faith in me. . . . I give you my word I will drop all research the moment I find what I am seeking."

"No, James, I implore you! Leave these things alone! Put them aside. . . . I'm going to tell you something that I ought not to tell you. . . . I assure you that if you don't abandon these dangerous paths of your own free will, you are going to be forced to abandon them. . . ."

"Oh? Have they been telling you something?" he

asked eagerly. "All the more reason for getting ahead fast! I'm going to make this test immediately."

"I will have no hand in it," I said. "Good-by!"

And I came away. But as soon as I was out in the street, I regretted my words.

XII

Next morning I received a message at my hotel. *Don't be obstinate* [it read]. *I was not quite myself. I have set free your protégés. Come over—you are the only man I can talk to about these things, and I need to talk about them. In any case, you are burning to know what has happened.—Yours,* H. B. J.

I jumped into a taxi, calling "Saint Barnaby's Hospital," to the driver. When I got there, the hospital porter, who by now had become a friend, told me where I could find James; he had just been called over to one of the wards. I went up, and from afar I could see his face of anguish lighten at the sight of me. Coming over to me, he took me affectionately by the arm.

"Be easy in your mind," he said. "I have broken those two globes. . . . But I missed you badly; I'll tell you why later on. . . . Just wait for me a few minutes."

He stepped behind the cretonne screen which had been placed round the bed of a woman patient for an examination, and I stood waiting. After a few minutes he reappeared, and led me on to the terrace.

"Well, James? Negative results?"

"Negative? Oh, no, not at all! Very curious results, but depressing."

"Depressing! You alarm me. . . . What happened?"

"Nothing serious. . . . But you remember how we both supposed that the fluid of the two globes would fill the whole of the available space? Well, that was a mistake! When I put the combined arrangement of the two sealed globes under the rays, only one, the upper one, was luminous."

"Really! But how do you explain that?"

"I don't explain, I never explain anything, I only state the facts. . . . The whole of the fluid in both globes, you see, had merged within the upper one. . . . Good. Well, now, tell me—do you suppose that this globe was a brighter or duller one than usual?"

"Brighter, of course, because it brought together——"

"Well, it wasn't! And that's what I find so depressing. . . . It was almost extinguished. . . . What is the deeper meaning of this phenomenon? What spiritual or sentimental reality can it point to? Perhaps we shall never know, either of us. . . . But faced with that wan, ashy light, those enfeebled and slowed-up currents, I thought of your scruples, and I saw more cogency in them than I did at first. . . . Even if there were only one chance in a million, I reflected, that two beings should be in misery through my own fault, yet that was ample reason for trying to save them. . . . You can imagine the strange and rather painful hour I went through. I kept repeating to myself the words of our friend Hamlet—'To die; to sleep; no more. . . .' I kept telling myself that after this hard life of ours, it is cruel to refuse men sleep and rest. . . . And at last I took a hammer, broke the tube, and turned the globe upward."

"And it emptied itself?"

"Of course."

"Bravo, James! I'm delighted! And I'd be even more so if you promised to leave things there. It seems to me that, having reached this point in your researches, and given the degree of precision they have attained, you have only two courses open: either you must make them public and repeat them in the presence of other scientists, or you must abandon them because you will be losing your position and your friends to no purpose. . . . As regards myself, I fear you will be losing me of necessity. My work is coming to an end, and I can't spend my life in England. In a fortnight I shall be leaving, and, believe me, I would leave with an easier mind if you gave me your word. . . ."

"Don't get sentimental, old man. A fortnight in France, and you will have forgotten me completely. . . . But you're right when you say that to continue repeating these experiments is useless, because nothing will persuade me to make them known. . . . I shall drop the whole thing. . . . Or at least, I'll only do one more . . . if circumstances ever make it possible. If that fails, the whole business will have been a dream, a dreary one, and no more. . . ."

"And you will give back Mr. Slutter his freedom?"

"You shall give it him yourself, this very evening."

And it was indeed myself who broke globe No. 1 that same evening. Before bringing myself to the point, I held it for a long time between my hands. In cracking it, would I be putting an end to the second, and brief, existence of Mr. William Slutter? There was no means of knowing, and it still seemed the lesser risk to allow nature to follow her accustomed course. I dropped the globe into an iron mortar, and with the noise of the splintering glass there was mingled, I fancied, a sort of infinitely distant vibration, infinitely faint, and yet perceptible.

* * *

When I saw Dr. Digby again I was able to assure him that James had abandoned the investigations which were disquieting the hospital authorities. Digby had already heard this from his informant, who was no doubt Gregory.

"I am pleased with this news," he said, "for we shouldn't have been able to shield him much longer."

I refrained from telling him that James had made a reservation in his promise for one eventuality. Yet I was almost certain that my friend, when he actually spoke those words, had a definite idea in his head; and, what is more, I thought I knew him well enough to have guessed at this idea. I had seen that the failure of that experiment in which he had tried to obtain the close commingling of two souls, or (as he would have said) two fluid "ghosts," had disappointed him profoundly, and that this disappointment was something far more than the disconcertment of a scientist whose hypothesis turns out to be unsound. It had long been noticeable that James's dominant emotion was an acutely painful sense of what the irremediable cleavage of death means for human beings. He had often spoken to me of those words one longs to have said, words to remain forever unspoken save to a dead body, blind and deaf. The possibility of a more enduring union between two souls was bound to attract him and touch him in his most sensitive spot. And now, instead of the enhanced vital force which he believed and hoped that he would find by producing that union in the strange world of his "ghosts," he had been faced with the contrary—the quenching of the united pair. But his desire was left unvanquished. He had certainly told himself that the failure was due to the fact of the beings thus brought together having been made to repel each other, and not to commingle. Furthermore, he thought that if two deeply united souls really could be combined, atom for atom, a superior state would then appear. Under his outward sarcasm, as I have already said, he was a sentimental. He believed profoundly in friendship, and in love. The single experiment of which he spoke would depend, I was certain, upon whether chance ever brought him two people, in their last moments, whose unity in life had been perfect: he would try to unite them once more in death.

You will think that the chance of this happening was small. I myself was not so sure. Unless one has lived right inside the life of a great town, as is possible for the police officer or the doctor to do, one has little idea of the sorrows and beauties it may hold. During the past two months I had been watching so many extraordinary cases pass through Saint Barnaby's that anything seemed possible. But my own stay in London was almost over, and I knew that if ever Dr. James carried out his last experiment, I should not be a witness of it. During that fortnight I saw him only once again. I was working hard. I had found an old French friend, a secretary at the Embassy, with whom I spent several evenings, and I did not return to Saint Barnaby's until the eve of my departure. I had telephoned to James asking if I could meet him, and he had sent word by the porter to come and see him in his own room about nine in the evening.

*   *   *

He was not there when I entered, so I took a book and sat down in the armchair. After a time, as there was no sign of James, I drew aside the curtain concealing the "ghosts." I hoped that he had completed their liberation, and I had an idea, if he had not already done it, of asking leave to carry out the act of release myself before leaving.

The globes were in their usual place, and to my great surprise I saw that there was a new one among them, bearing on its label the number "10-11," without any name. I instantly realized that James had repeated the experiment of fusion which had angered me, and I felt seriously annoyed with him. . . . "10-11.". . . No name. . . . Who were these two hapless creatures? I was filled with a vague sense of anxiety which I had difficulty in defining more exactly. . . . Why wasn't James coming back? He had given me a definite rendezvous, and to be seriously late was not like him.

I was turning the mysterious ball over and over on my knees, when I felt two hands laid on my shoulder. "Alas, poor Yorick!" came a gay cheerful voice. I turned around, and was astonished by the change I saw in James's face. Never had I seen a human being so completely transformed within a few days. The lines of his face, usually restless and twitching, had taken a look of soothed serenity. His smile was no longer a sarcasm but a relaxation.

"What's happened to you, James?"

"Happened? To me? Nothing. . . . Why?"

"You look so happy. . . ."

"Oh! Is that so obvious then? Well the truth is that I am—and I'll show you why. . . . Just put that globe you have there on the mantelpiece, will you? How gloomily you were gazing at it! That's right. . . . Now help me to get my apparatus out from this corner. . . . Thanks. . . . Just a bit to the left. . . . Will you turn the lights out?"

I turned the switch, and a cry escaped me in spite

of myself. A sphere of light was gleaming on the mantelpiece with prodigious radiance. It could hardly be compared with anything but that of a full moon in a perfectly clear summer sky in Greece or the East. It was a gleaming pearl, and its depths moved currents more gleaming still, and a whirling nebula of liquid, flaming diamond.

"Marvelous!" I said. . . . "But what miracle—"

For a few minutes longer he let me contemplate this amazing spectacle, and then, after putting on the lights in the room, he told me the story. It appeared that in a neighboring music hall, two acrobats, the Hanley Brothers, had been performing their flying trapeze act during the past fortnight. James had not seen their "turn," but Digby, who had seen it, described it to him, and later told me, too, about it. He had considered it as a spectacle of most uncommon quality and gracefulness. Ned and Fred Hanley were two very handsome young men, really brothers, whose resemblance was in itself a marvel. For their turn a backcloth of black velvet was dropped, and against this, during their terrifying spinning, their two white bodies stood out under the beams of the spotlight.

The brothers had enjoyed a great success, so great indeed that the management asked them to extend their engagement to another week. What happened on the first night of that extension? Nobody knew, and the police were making inquiries. Whatever the cause, one of the supporting wires of the trapezes had given, and the two brothers had fallen from a great height. Seriously injured, they were taken to the hospital and died there during the night, only a few minutes between them.

"Some of their friends came along with them," said James, "and I heard them talking about the extraordinary unison between these two lads, their work in common, and the strength of the affection that joined them; and I could not then withstand my desire to carry out in such favorable circumstances the final experiment I spoke about. . . . Don't worry —Gregory wasn't there; I had the help of a laboratory lad who understood nothing of what he was doing. . . . I came back to my room at three o'clock this morning; I united these two ghosts, and was able to contemplate the wonderful sight you have just been admiring yourself. . . . Do you now advise me to break that globe?"

"No, my dear James. I can only guess what is happening in it, but it would be surprising if such great beauty were not a sign of happiness."

And then, as the hour was getting late, I had to explain, notwithstanding my desire to stay, that I had come to say good-by.

"True," said James. "Well, then, good-by. . . . I don't know if I shall see you again. When life cuts apart it cuts deeply. But I shall always be grateful to you for these months during which you have been a loyal and discreet friend to me. . . . So loyal and discreet, indeed, that I am going to ask one last favor of you. . . . It won't be immediate—perhaps it will never arise. But it is possible that a day will come when I shall need your help. . . . Where I shall be, I know not, but I shall send you a telegram asking you to join me by the most rapid means, whatever your engagements at the moment. . . . You know me well enough to realize that I would not make such an extraordinary request if I did not have grave reason. . . . I give you my pledge to make only one such appeal to you in the course of your life, but for this single occasion I ask for your solemn oath."

"You have it," I said, moved by his deep earnestness.

"God bless you!" he answered.

He came with me to the door. It was a fine summer evening; but the moon in the starry sky shone with less brilliance than the light I had just seen on the mantelpiece, twofold and alive.

XIII

When James said that I would forget him, I protested to the contrary. But he was not far wrong. During the next few years my work made heavy demands on me, and did not bring me back to England. Sometimes I thought about those strange weeks, but as one thinking of some fantastic tale rather than of a real memory. The first letter I had from James was early in 1926, to tell me that he had kept his

promise and renounced the fuller pursuit of his researches; the second, in October, 1927, was to let me
know that Miss Philipps had lost her father and that
he was about to marry her. This did not really
astonish me. I sent them a small present, and in her
letter of thanks, Edith Philipps, or rather Edith
James, told me that she needed a few months' rest
in the south of France, that her husband was taking
a holiday to accompany her, and that they would
both be coming through Paris the following week.
Unfortunately, I was in the country when this letter
arrived, and I did not see my friends when they were
passing through.

In December I had a card from James. He and
his wife were at Cap-Martin. He asked whether I
would not come and pay them a visit, if I had any
thought of traveling that winter, or if not, whether a
telegram from him would still find me in Paris. I replied that, barring unforeseen events, I was anxious
to remain at home and work.

About the middle of January, 1928, a friend of
mine, a man of letters, fell ill and asked me to take
his place for a lecture which he had engaged to give
at Copenhagen. To oblige him, I accepted; and it
may be that the memory of Hilda James, whose story
I had not forgotten, counted for something in my
desire to see something of Denmark. My journey was
only to take five days in all.

I arrived in Copenhagen in the morning, and had
to speak the same night. As soon as I got out of the

train, one of my welcomers handed me a telegram which had just arrived for me. I opened it and read: "Come. James. Florida, Cap-Martin."

I was bowled over. It had not occurred to me to let James know of my being away for such a brief time. But he had counted on my pledge, and my mind was made up to keep it, although circumstances would force me to do so more slowly than I could have wished. To the great surprise and annoyance of the organizers of the lecture, I told them my dearest friend was dying, and that I would have to set off home again. What time was the first train? There was none before the next morning.

I spent my day in scanning timetables with the hotel porter. Even granted that there was no hitch, and that none of my trains on this long journey was late, I could not reach James until the third day. But his telegram, forwarded from Paris, was already twenty-four hours old; my friend would think me singularly careless. I inquired about the possibility of going by air, but the weather was bad and the winter service uncertain. All I could do was to send James a wire in my turn, explaining my delay and announcing my arrival. This I did. I lectured that evening, better than usual because of my high pitch of excitement; I did not sleep, and left Copenhagen in the morning.

During the long ensuing hours of Danish and German and French trains, ferryboats, customs and passports, I tried vainly to foresee what I would find at my journey's end. I was filled with mournful and inevitable forebodings. The sole link of real intimacy between James and myself, and the one which made me, so far as he was concerned, irreplaceable, was that macabre quest of which I had been the witness. If he was urgently in need of seeing me, it could only be to help him in the course of an experiment of the same kind; and as his anxiety about it was such that he summoned me, it was not hard to guess what this experiment might be. Would I get there in time? Wouldn't James and I have difficulties with the local authorities? I remembered with relief that M. Raibaldi, the *préfet* of Alpes-Maritimes, was a friend of my father's. He might be useful. Down came the train, past the olive trees, alongside the pebbly streams. Beyond Marseilles, the vivid blue of the sea and the white sails seemed cheerless and frightening. And at last, under a summer sun, about half-past two in the afternoon, as I was in despair of ever arriving, the train stopped in the station of Roquebrune-Cap-Martin.

James was not at the station. This hardly surprised me, for he could not have known which train I would arrive by, so I took a cab and drove to his villa. It was a small pavilion ringed with palm trees, in a garden full of flowers. I remember my pleasure at a whiff of heliotrope that reached me when I was ringing the bell. A servant clothed in black appeared on the steps of the house. 'I seem to know this man,' I thought, as he came across the garden to open the gate for me. 'Where the deuce have I seen him?' And just as he reached me I recognized him. It was Biggs, an English soldier who had been the doctor's batman during the War, and whose services I myself had shared with James for several months.

"Good day, sir," he answered. "Yes, my wife and I were here, with Dr. and Mrs. James. . . . I am sorry to tell you, sir, that the doctor is dead. Did you not receive my second wire?"

"No. . . . Dead? James? But when? I heard from him only four days ago.

"He was already dead, sir. . . . But come in."

He took my bag and carried it with him into the house. Then, seating me on a garden chair, he told me this story.

"You know, sir, that Mrs. James has always been very ill. She had an operation shortly before her father's death. . . . When she became the doctor's wife, it was obvious to everyone that she was dying, and of course to a medical man as he was, more obvious than to anyone. . . . I always said, sir, that the doctor was a saint, and only married Miss Philipps to be better able to look after her. When he suggested that I should take service with them and come with them to France, I said to my wife, 'It won't be a lasting place, but we must take it. . . .' And we haven't regretted it, sir. . . . Nobody could have been nicer than the doctor and his wife. They were very fond of each other. . . . Never did I see people so easily happy. In the daytime, when the weather was good, they went and sat on the beach together, and in the evenings the doctor read aloud. . . .

"For the first couple of months Mrs. James was pretty well. But after that, from the middle of December, she seemed only to get paler and more silent. . . . It was obviously the beginning of the end. But happily the doctor kept her hoping right to the last that he would pull her around. He told her he was going to give her a new treatment he had invented. . . . And in one room he prepared some very strange contrivances for this purpose. There was a big glass bell which could be raised and lowered by moving a small lever, small flasks, and an apparatus covered with a black cloth. . . . His 'laboratory,' Doctor called that room. . . . My wife and I never entered it. . . . What's more, he never used it himself, except— But I'm forgetting to tell you the most important thing, sir. Five days ago Mrs. James had a fainting fit and remained unconscious. My wife was with her, along with the doctor. About one o'clock in the morning he told my wife to go to bed, and that he would call her down if he needed her. He did not call her, and about eight next morning she came back into the room. . . . There she was startled to find that Mrs. James was no longer in her bed, and that the doctor had disappeared. On the table there was a large envelope addressed to me. . . . My wife was frightened and brought it to me in a hurry. I read the poor doctor's letter. . . . Here it is, sir. . . ."

Biggs drew two letters from his pocket and handed me one. I read it:

"Biggs—you are to do exactly what I am telling you, extraordinary as it may appear to you. Mrs. James died this morning, and I wish to avoid surviving her. Our two bodies are in the room I called my laboratory. Do not go in, and do not touch anything. Send off the telegram which you will find in the envelope; it is for the French officer who was with us at Ypres. He will come instantly and make all arrangements. So do not concern yourself with anything. Simply send off the telegram and wait. All will be well. Good-by."

"But then, Biggs . . . ," I began.

"Just a moment, sir. There was another letter, addressed to yourself, which I was to give you as soon as you arrived."

I felt a touch of reproach in his tone of voice. The letter he handed me was sealed. I tore it open and read as follows:

"I fear I shall cause you pain, and probably serious trouble; but I have your promise, and know that you will do what I ask of you. Biggs will explain what has happened—I had foreseen it for a long time. You will then understand (although I dare say you had already done so), why during the time you were in London, I was so feverish in pushing forward the researches which seemed so wild to you. In the house you are about to enter you will find a laboratory very much like that in which we worked together at Saint

Barnaby's. Under the glass bell jar in the center you will see two bodies—my wife's and my own. You remember the way in which the globe at the top of the jar is taken off. Do so with care. Then, after sealing up the globe, take it over in front of the black apparatus familiar to you. I hope that you will then have a glimpse of something of Edith and myself. If you find, as I hope, and believe you will, our ghosts mingled in the same way as those of the two brothers whom you doubtless remember, it is my wish that you should preserve them, and if possible that you should provide for their safekeeping, by your children, and your children's children. Naturally, I cannot hope for the very long preservation of so fragile an object; but in my earthly existence I have had too brief an enjoyment of my poor Edith's love. If, thanks to you, I can find a few years' happiness in a world that is still outside our conception, I think you will have done a good deed. . . ."

With that sentence I broke off reading, and eagerly asked Biggs:

"And where are the doctor and his wife now?"

"At the cemetery, sir. . . . After sending you the telegram I waited two days. . . . And then as there was no sign of you, my wife and I got frightened. . . . What could we say if we were asked why we had left these two dead people unburied? We're in foreign parts. . . . I only know a few words of French. . . . I went to the *Mairie,* sir, and showed them the doctor's letter—mine, not yours. A doctor came up, and broke the glass."

"Broke the glass! Then everything's ruined, Biggs.
. . . But why break it, when you told me it was easy
to lift?"

"I don't know, sir, I didn't understand what he
said. . . . I think that when he came in and saw these
two bodies under a glass cover, he thought it was a
case of asphyxiation. . . . Later on, after the post-
mortem, he told me that the doctor had taken poison.
. . . At least, I think that's how it was, sir—as I say,
I didn't understand very well. . . . But what could
the doctor expect, sir? And if you had arrived sooner.
. . . After all, he was dead—what *could* we have
done?"

Interrupting, I asked him to take me to the laboratory. I clung to a faint hope that perhaps, by some
miracle, the globe had remained intact at the top of
the bell jar. Alas, I found the room strewn with
broken glass. Of the jar and the globe there remained
nothing but fragments. Those who had found the
bodies had no doubt wanted to waste no time. They
could hardly be blamed; how could they have guessed
the strange nature of what they were wrecking?

"There is also this case, sir. The doctor had fixed a
label on it saying that I was to give it to you. So I
hid it in my own room when the men came from the
Mairie."

"What's in the box, Biggs?"

"I don't know, sir."

I opened it. On a layer of crumpled paper I found
a glass globe just like those of Saint Barnaby's, and
I picked it up with sudden hope. Then I saw that it

bore a label which I knew well: "10-11, NED AND FRED HANLEY."

"Poor James!" I reflected. "So he succeeded in giving to others the survival he would so gladly have had for himself!"

I went over to the cemetery to lay some flowers on the graves of Edith and Howard Bruce James, and left for Paris that same evening, carrying on my knees the case bequeathed to me by my friend. I clung to the object with a superstitious care which was the greater for my vague sense of remorse. Certainly, I knew not what form of existence James had desired for himself and his beloved, but I had given him my word to secure it for him; and now, in spite of myself but still through my failure, he was robbed of the fruit of his researches. Endlessly I wondered what I ought to have done. Should I have warned James before I left for Copenhagen? There had been no time; and in any case, though I had always guessed more or less what he hoped from me, I had not fully realized it. It had not occurred to me that James would want to die at the same time as his wife. Was I to be solely responsible for that lack of comprehension? He alone knew his own designs, and could he not have anticipated more methodically all the opposing hazards in this unique event? Couldn't he have given Biggs exact instructions in the event of my not arriving? But doubtless he had thought that Biggs would grasp none of such recommendations, or would be a poor hand in carrying out a delicate maneuver. And in the end, as I reached Paris, I told myself that these broodings over the past were vain.

For a long time I deliberately refrained from thinking about the experiments at Saint Barnaby's and their tragic climax. But for some months I have been feeling ill and quite near death myself. I have felt it my duty to leave an account of the incredible and true facts of which fortune made me the witness. It is my only means of providing for the safekeeping, with all the care I have always taken myself, of the globe containing the mingled ghosts of Ned and Fred Hanley. Last night, possibly for the last time, I had a fancy to look at them in the invisible beam of the apparatus which was the doctor's legacy. Their brightness has not dimmed since the day when it made me cry out in admiration, up in James's room. The amazing persistence of so beautiful a phenomenon only heightens my grief at having been unable to unite, in that same way, Edith James and her husband.

The glass globe will be found in the small cabinet, shut off by a blue curtain behind a grille, on the right-hand side of my desk.

The

Earth

Dwellers

The

Earth

Dwellers

Fragment From a Universal History Published by The University of * * * in 1992.

BY THE END of 1970 friendly relations had been established between the Earth and most of the major planets, and terrestrial scientists became anxious to compare their own hypotheses and doctrines with those of their colleagues in other worlds. But such comparisons were often difficult, because, as is well known, the eminent physicists of Venus, Jupiter, and Mars had no perception of either light or sound, and lived in a world of radiations of which we had hitherto been quite ignorant. But the theory of sensorial equivalents made rapid progress, and at the date of writing (1992) it may be said that we are capable of transposing every language of the planetary system into Earth language—except Saturnian.

One of the most interesting discoveries due to this new philology was that of books written about ourselves, the Earth Dwellers, by the scientists of foreign planets. Mankind had not the slightest idea that for millions of years past he had been under observation, thanks to instruments very much more powerful than his own, by the naturalists of Venus, Mars, and even Uranus. Terrestrial science lagged far behind the science of neighboring bodies, and as our organs were insensitive to the radiations utilized by these observers, it was impossible for us to know that, in the most secret moments of our lives, we were sometimes within the field of vision of a celestial ultramicroscope.

Nowadays these works can be consulted by any scholar in the library of the League of Planets. They provide most commendable reading for young men eager to devote themselves to the learned sciences, not only because of their great intrinsic interest, but also because of the sense of humility which they cannot fail to evoke. To observe the incredible errors made by beings of such high intelligence and so wonderfully equipped for research, one cannot refrain from reverting to a number of our own human affirmations, wondering whether we have not observed plants and animals very much as the Martians observed us.

One case in particular strikes us as worthy of careful study: that of the Uranian scholar A.E. 17, who published his book, *Man and His Life,* in 1959.[1] Until the War that book was the standard work not only in Uranus but also, in translations, among the inhabitants of Venus and Mars. To ourselves it is readily accessible because, alone among our fellow-planetaries, the Uranians share with us the sense of sight, which makes their vocabulary approximate closely to ours. Moreover, the experiments carried out by A.E. 17 were such as completely to upset the Earth throughout a period of six months; and we have access to the terrestrial account of these events in the newspapers and memoirs of the time.

We propose here:

(*a*) To describe briefly a few of the events noted on our own planet in the year 1954;

(*b*) to show what interpretation the eminent A.E. 17 put on his own experiments.

THE MYSTERIOUS SPRINGTIME

In the month of March, 1954, numerous observers throughout the northern hemisphere gave surprising reports of atmospheric conditions. Notwithstanding fine and cool weather, storms of the utmost violence were bursting suddenly within strictly limited zones. Ships' captains and airplane pilots reported to the Central Meteorological Bureau that their compasses had for several seconds behaved quite

[1] Original Uranian edition, 1959. First terrestrial edition, 1982.

wildly for no conceivable reason. In several places, under a clear sky, people saw what appeared to be the shadow of a huge cloud passing over the ground, although no such cloud was visible. The newspapers published interviews with the eminent meteorologists, who explained that they had anticipated this phenomenon, which was due to sunspots and would come to an end with the equinoctial tides. But the advent of the equinox only brought stranger happenings in its wake.

THE "HYDE PARK HILL" INCIDENT

On the third Sunday in April, the crowds of men and women listening to the open-air orators giving their pitch at Marble Arch, suddenly saw passing overhead the shadow of an invisible obstacle mysteriously interposed between the Earth and the sun. A few seconds later, from the park railings to a point some three or four hundred yards inside the park, there occurred an abrupt upheaval of the ground. Trees were uprooted and pedestrians tumbled over and were buried, while those who were on the edge of the disturbed area were dumfounded to observe that a great funnel at least three hundred feet deep had been scooped out, the soil from which had been thrown up to form a hill of corresponding height.

A policeman, giving evidence next day at the inquest on victims, said, "It all happened just as if a giant had been wielding a spade in the park. Yes, it was just like someone using a spade, because the outer edge of the cavity was trim and smooth, while the edge on the side where the hill came consisted of crumbling loose soil, with half-cut heads and bodies protruding from it."

Over three hundred citizens walking in the park had been buried alive. Some who had only been covered with a light layer of earth managed to extricate themselves with difficulty. Some, too, suddenly lost their senses and rushed down the steep slope of the new hill, uttering dreadful shrieks. On the summit of the mound there appeared the upright figure of a Salvation Army preacher, Colonel R. W. Ward, who, with astonishing presence of mind, still shaking the dirt from his hair and clothing, began to bellow: "I told you so, brothers! You have sacrificed to false gods, and now the Lord God is angered with his people, and the hand of the Lord God has fallen heavy upon us. . . ."

And indeed this inexplicable event bore such a likeness to certain divine punishments as described in Holy Writ that skeptics among the bystanders were instantly converted, and began lives of practicing religion to which they have from that moment been steadfast.

The episode enabled people to appreciate the virtues of the Metropolitan Police. Three members of the force were among the victims, but a dozen others, arriving instantly on the scene, set to work at digging with great courage. Telephone messages were sent out at once to the military authorities and fire stations, and General Clarkwell, the Commissioner of Police, took command of the rescue forces, and within four hours Hyde Park had resumed its normal appearance. Unfortunately, the dead numbered two hundred.

Scientists gave the most varied explanations of the disaster. The theory of an earthquake, the only reasonable one if the supernatural were ruled out, did not seem plausible, for no shock had been recorded by any seismograph. The public was fairly well satisfied when the experts informed them that it *had* been an earthquake, but an earthquake of a very special sort which they had labeled a "vertical-montiform seismic variant."

THE HOUSE IN THE AVENUE
VICTOR HUGO

The Hyde Park incident was followed by a considerable number of similar occurrences, which attracted much less public attention because they caused no human fatalities. But at different points these strange mounds were seen taking shape with the same swiftness, each of them bordered by a precipice with sheer, clean-cut fall. In certain places these hills are still in existence: as for instance the one in the plain of Ayen in Périgord, that of Roznov in Wallachia, and that of Itapura in Brazil.

But the mysterious spade which was thus apparently wielded on bare land was now, alas, to attack human erections.

About midday on April 24, a strange noise, compared by some who heard it to that of a whizzing blade, by others to that of an extremely fine and powerful water jet, astonished the passers-by in the region of Paris bounded approximately by the Arc de Triomphe, the Avenue de la Grande Armée, the Avenue Marceau, and the Avenue Henri Martin.

People happening to be opposite the building known as 66 Avenue Victor Hugo saw an enormous oblique cleft appear across it; the house was shaken by two or three tremors, and suddenly the whole of the top story, occupied by the servants' rooms, seemed to crumble away as if under powerful pressure. The frenzied inhabitants appeared at the windows and on the balconies. Fortunately, although the building was literally cut in two, it did not collapse. Halfway up the staircase the rescuers came upon the fissure produced by the invisible instrument. It looked exactly as if a blade had cut through the wood of the steps, the carpet, the metal balustrade, following a line at right angles to these. Everything in its path—furniture, carpets, pictures, books—had been cut in two with a clean stroke, very neatly. By a miracle nobody was injured. A girl sleeping on the third floor found her bed sliced obliquely across; but the cut had just missed her. She had felt no pain, but did experience a shock like that of a weak electric battery.

In this case, too, there were numerous explanations. The word "seismic" was again produced. Certain newspapers accused the architect and proprietor of the building of having used faulty materials in its construction. A communist deputy raised the question in the Chamber.

THE TRANSPORTATION PHENOMENA

Like the Hyde Park occurrence, the accident in the Avenue Victor Hugo was followed by several almost identical in kind, which we shall not recount, but which ought, as we now see, to have convinced observant minds of a hidden will engaged in the furtherance of a definite plan. In numerous countries, houses, great and small, were sundered by an invisible force. Several farmhouses, one in Massachusetts, another in Denmark, another in Spain, were raised into the air and dropped back on to the ground, smashed to pieces with their inhabitants. The French Building in New York was cut in two. About fifty men and women met their deaths in these occurrences, but as they took place in very different countries, each isolated case being responsible only for a few victims, and also as nobody could provide an explanation, very little was said about them.

It was different with the subsequent series of happenings, which kept the whole planet in a ferment of excitement throughout May and June, 1954. The first victim was a young Negress of Hartford, Connecticut, who was leaving her employers' house one morning when a postman, the sole witness of the accident, saw her suddenly soar into the air, uttering terrible cries. She rose to a height of three hundred feet and then crashed to the ground. The postman declared that he had seen no aerial apparatus of any sort overhead.

The second case of "transportation" was that of a customs official at Calais, who was also seen rising vertically and disappearing at high speed toward the English coast. A few minutes later he was found on the Dover cliffs, dead, but with no visible injuries. He looked as if he had been laid gently down on the ground; he was blue, like a man hanged.

Then began the period of the so-called "successful transportations." The first victim to arrive living at the end of his journey was an aged beggar, who was seized by an invisible hand when he was begging for alms in front of Notre Dame, and ten minutes later was deposited in the middle of Piccadilly Circus at the feet of a stupefied policeman. He had not suffered at all, and had the impression of having been conveyed in a closed cabin to which neither wind nor light could penetrate. Eyewitnesses of his departure had observed that he became invisible immediately after he was raised from the ground.

For several weeks longer these "transportations" continued. Once they were known to be quite harmless, they were regarded as rather comical. The choice of the invisible hand seemed to be completely whimsical. Once it was a little girl of Denver, Colorado, who found herself set down in a Russian steppe; another time a Saragossa dentist turned up in Stockholm. The "transportation" which caused most talk was that of the venerable President of the French Senate, M. Paul Reynaud, who was picked up in the Luxembourg Gardens and deposited on the shore of Lake Ontario. He took the opportunity of making a journey through Canada, was triumphantly welcomed back at the Bois de Boulogne station, and this unsought publicity was probably largely responsible for his election as President of the Republic, in 1956.

It should be noted that, after their journeys, the subjects of "transportation" were smeared with a reddish liquid that stained their clothing, for no ascertainable reason. This was the only inconvenience of these otherwise harmless adventures. After about two months they ceased, to be followed by a new and still stranger series which began with the famous episode of the "Two Couples."

THE "TWO COUPLES" EPISODE

The first of the two famous couples was a French one, living in a small house close to Paris, in Neuilly. The husband, Jacques Martin, was on the teaching staff of the Lycée Pasteur, a sporting and scholarly young man, and the author of a remarkable bio-

graphical study on Paul Morand. He and his wife had four children. On July 3, toward midnight, Mme. Martin had just fallen asleep when she heard that steamlike whistling which we have already mentioned, felt a slight shaking, and had the impression of being very rapidly raised into the air. Opening her eyes, she was stupefied to see that the pale light of the moon was flooding her room, a whole wall of which had vanished, that she was lying on the edge of a bed cut in two, and that on her left hand, where her husband had been lying a few seconds before, there was a bottomless gulf, above which the stars were glittering. She flung herself in terror toward the still solid edge of the bed, and was amazed (and at the same time reassured) to find that it did not wobble, although it was left with only two legs. Mme. Martin felt that she was rising no higher, but was being moved very fast in a straight line; then she was made aware, by a feeling in the heart like that which one has in a lift descending too quickly, that she was dropping. Imagining that her fall would end with a crash, she had already closed her eyes in anticipation of the final shock. But it was gentle and elastic, and when she looked around her, she could see nothing. The room was dark. Her own narrative continues:

"I put out my arm; everything was solid. The abyss had apparently closed up again. I called my husband's name, thinking that I had been passing through a nightmare and feeling anxious to tell him about it. My groping hand felt a man's arm, and I heard a strong unknown voice say in English, 'Oh, my dear, what a fright you gave me!' I started back and wanted to turn on the light, but I could not find the electric switch. 'What's wrong?' said the unknown. He himself turned on a light. We both uttered simultaneous cries. In front of me was a fair-haired young Englishman, with a small short nose, rather shortsighted, and still half asleep, in blue pajamas. Down the middle of the bed ran a crack; sheets, mattress and bolster were all cut in two. There was a difference of three or four inches in the level of the two portions of the bed.

"When my bedfellow had recovered his wits, his demeanor in these difficult circumstances gave me a high opinion of the British race. After a short but very excusable moment of confusion, his correctness was as complete and natural as if we had been in a drawing room. I spoke his language and told him my name. He told me that his was John Graham. The place we were in was Richmond. Looking around, I saw that the whole of one half of my own room had accompanied me; I recognized my window with its cherry-colored curtains, the large photograph of my husband, the small table with books beside my bed, and even my watch on top of my books. The other half, Mr. Graham's, was unknown to me. On the bedside table there were a portrait of a very pretty woman, photographs of children, some magazines, and a box of cigarettes. John Graham looked at me for a very long time, examining the background against which I had appeared to him, and then said with the utmost seriousness, 'What are you doing here?' I explained that I knew nothing about it, and, pointing to the large portrait, I said, 'This is my husband.' Pointing likewise, he answered, 'This is my wife.' She was delightful, and the disturbing thought came to me that she was perhaps at that very moment in the arms of Jacques. 'Do you suppose,' I asked him, 'that half of your house has been transported to France at the same time as half of ours has come here?' 'Why?' he said. He annoyed me. Why, indeed? I knew nothing about it at all. . . . Because this affair had a sort of natural symmetry of its own.

" 'A queer business,' he said, shaking his head. 'How can it be possible?' 'It isn't possible,' I said, 'but it has happened.'

"At this moment cries were heard apparently coming from upstairs, and the same thought struck us: 'The children?' John Graham jumped out of bed and ran barefoot toward a door, the door of *his* half. He opened it, and I could hear cries, the sound of coughing, and then the Englishman's powerful voice mingling oaths with words of comfort. I made haste to rise, and looked in the mirror. My face looked just as usual. I then noticed that my nightdress was décolleté and looked around for my kimono; but I remembered having hung it in the half of the room which had stayed behind. Standing there in front of the mirror, I heard a pitiable voice behind me.

"The cries in the nursery were redoubled, weeping and appeals mingling with them.

" 'Come and help me,' he said in a beseeching tone.

" 'Of course I will . . . but have you got your wife's dressing gown, and slippers?'

" 'Oh, yes, of course. . . .'

"Handing me his own dressing gown he showed me the way to the nursery. The children were splendid. I managed to soothe them. It was the youngest, a lovely fair baby, who seemed to be suffering most. I comforted him as best I could, and took his hand; he accepted my presence.

"In this way we spent a couple of hours in that room, both in a state of mental anguish, he thinking of his wife, and I of my husband.

"I asked if we could not telephone to the police. He tried, and found that his telephone had been cut off; his radio aerial had also been cut; the house must have been looking extremely odd. When dawn appeared, Mr. Graham went out. The children had fallen asleep. In a few minutes he returned for me, saying that really the front of the house was well worth looking at. And it was! The unknown contriver of this miracle had evidently wanted to pick two houses of the same height divided in the same way, and he had succeeded; but the styles were so different that the combined effect took one's breath away. Our house at Neuilly was of brick, very plain, its tall windows framed with stone; the English house was a small black and white cottage, with wide bay windows. The juxtaposition of these two utterly

different halves formed a most ludicrous ensemble—
like a harlequin of Picasso's.

"I urged Mr. Graham to put on his clothes and
send off a telegram to France to find out what had
happened to his wife. He told me that the telegraph
office did not open till eight o'clock. He was a stolid
creature, apparently incapable of conceiving that in
such peculiar circumstances one could infringe on
regulations and awaken the telegraph clerk. I shook
him energetically, but in vain. All I could get out of
him was: 'It only opens at eight.' In the end, about
seven o'clock, just when he was going out, we saw a
policeman arriving. He was gazing at the house in
amazement, and had brought a telegram from the
head of the Paris police, asking if I was there and
announcing that Mrs. John Graham was safe and
sound at Neuilly."

It is not worth while continuing the quotation of
this narrative *in extenso*. Suffice it to say that Mrs.
Graham tended Mme. Martin's children as devotedly
as the latter did the little English ones, that both
couples declared themselves charmed by the ami-
ability of their companions in adventure, and that
both households remained close friends to their dying
days. Mme. Martin was still alive ten years ago, in her
family home at Chambourcy (Seine-et-Oise).

* * *

The space allotted to this chapter in the general
plan of this volume does not allow us to recount the

analogous adventures which astonished mankind throughout that month of August, 1954.

The series of "sliced houses" was even longer than that of the "transportations." Over one hundred couples were interchanged in this way, and the changes became a favorite theme with novelists and film writers. An element of whimsical sensuality which was much to the public's taste continued. Besides, it was diverting to see (as it really happened) a queen waking up in a policeman's bed, and a ballet girl in that of the President of the United States. Then the series stopped dead, and gave place to another. It looked as if the mysterious beings who amused themselves by disturbing the lives of humans were capricious, and quick to tire of their games.

THE CAGING

Early in September, the hand whose power was by now known to all the world fell upon some of the finest minds on its surface. A dozen men, nearly all chemists or physicists, men of the highest achievement, were simultaneously abstracted from different points among the civilized countries and transported to a clearing in the Forest of Fontainebleau.

A group of lads, who had come there in the early hours of the morning to climb the rocks, noticed some old men wandering forlornly among the trees. Seeing that they were in difficulties, the young men tried to approach them to offer help, but were taken aback to find themselves suddenly checked by some transparent but insurmountable resistance. They tried to find a way around the obstacle, but after making a complete circle around the clearing they realized that it was completely ringed by an invisible rampart. One of the scientists was recognized by a few of the youths as their professor, and they called him by name. He did not seem to hear them. Sound could not penetrate the barrier. The celebrated personages were there like caged beasts.

Before very long they seemed to accept the situation. They were observed to be lying down in the sunlight; and then, drawing pieces of paper from their pockets, they began scribbling mathematical formulas and arguing quite cheerfully. One of the young onlookers went off to inform the authorities, and by noon many curious spectators were beginning to come on the scene. By noon the scientists were showing signs of anxiety; they were all of advanced years, and they dragged themselves rather wearily to the edge of the ring, where, seeing that their voices were not reaching anyone, they made signs that they should be supplied with food.

A few officers were present, and one of them had what appeared to be the excellent notion of supplying the unfortunate men with supplies by airplane. A couple of hours later the drone of a motor was heard, and the pilot, passing skillfully over the circular clearing, dropped some packages of food exactly over the center. But, unfortunately, about sixty feet above the ground the packages were seen to stop in their fall, bounce back, and then were left suspended in midair. The cage had a roof composed of the same invisible radiations.

Toward nightfall the old men became desperate, signaling that they were dying of hunger and dreaded the night chills. The anguished onlookers could do nothing for them. Were they going to witness the perishing of this remarkable assemblage of great intellects?

In the pale light of the dawn it was at first thought that the situation had not changed, but closer examination showed that quite a new setting had appeared in the center of the "cage." The invisible hand had staged things so that the packages dropped by the airplane were now suspended at the end of rope about fifteen feet above the ground, while alongside this rope hung another which actually reached the ground. To any young man it would have been an easy matter to swing himself up and reach the packages that held the hopes of safety. But unhappily there was little likelihood that any of these venerable men of learning could undertake this difficult gymnastic feat. They were seen walking around the ropes and gauging their strength, but none of them ventured further.

A whole day went by in this way. Night fell. Gradually the curious throng melted away. About midnight one young student took it into his head to ascertain whether the barrier of radiations still held. To his great surprise he found nothing barring his way, walked straight on, and uttered a cry of triumph. The cruel powers which had made men their toys for two whole days were consenting to spare their victims. The scientists were fed and warmed, and none of them succumbed.

*   *   *

Such are the chief facts which distinguished this period, at the time inexplicable, but which we now know to have corresponded to a period of experiments on the planet Uranus. We shall now give a few extracts, in our opinion the most interesting, from the book of the famous A.E. 17.

The reader will understand that we have been obliged to find terrestrial equivalents for the Uranian words, and the translation is only approximate. Uranian time consists of years very much longer than ours, and wherever possible we have made a transposition into terrestrial time. Furthermore, to designate ourselves the Uranians use a word which signifies, roughly, "apterous bipeds"; but this is needlessly complicated, and we have in most places substituted the words "men" or "Earth Dwellers." Similarly, we have translated the queer word by which they designated our cities by the word "manheaps," which gives in our view a fair suggestion of the associations of analogous ideas. Finally, the reader should not overlook the fact that the Uranian, although endowed like ourselves with the sense of sight, is ignorant of sound. Uranians commnunicate with each other by means of a special organ consisting of a series of small colored lamps which flash on and off. Observing that men were without this organ, and being unable to imagine speech, the Uranian naturally supposed that we were incapable of communicating our ideas to each other.

Here we can offer only a few brief excerpts from the book by A.E. 17 on *Man and His Life*. But we strongly advise the student to read the book in its entirety; there is an excellent school edition published with appendix and notes by Professor Fischer of Peking.

* * *

MAN AND HIS LIFE

By

A.E. 17

When the surface of the small planets, particularly that of the Earth, is examined through an ordinary telescope, large stains may be noticed, more streaky in texture than those formed by a lake or ocean. If these stains are observed over a long enough period, they are seen to expand throughout several terrestrial centuries, pass through a period of maximum size, and then diminish, or even in some cases disappear. Many observers have thought that they were related to some unhealthy condition of the soil. And indeed nothing could be more like the development and reabsorption of a tumor in an organism. But with the invention of the ultratelemicroscope, it has been possible to detect that we are here confronted by an accumulation of living matter. The imperfections of the first apparatus did not allow us to see more than a confused swarming, a sort of throbbing jelly, and excellent observers, such as A. 33, then maintained that these terrestrial colonies were composed of animals joined to each other and living a common existence. With our present apparatus it is at once obvious that things are quite otherwise. The individual creatures can be clearly distinguished, and their movements can be followed. The stains observed by A. 33 are in point of fact huge nests which can almost be compared to Uranian cities and are known to us as "manheaps."

The minute animals inhabiting these towns, Men, are apterous biped animals, with an indifferent electrical system, and generally provided with an artificial epidermis. It was long believed that they secreted this supplementary skin themselves. But my researches enable me to declare that this is not so; they are impelled by a powerful instinct to collect certain animal or vegetable fibers and assemble them in such a way as to form a protection against cold.

I use the word "instinct," and from the outset of

this work I must lay stress on a clear indication of my feelings regarding a question which ought never to have been raised and has, especially during recent years, been treated with incredible levity. A curious mode of thought has become habitual among our younger naturalists, in attributing to these terrestrial vegetations an intelligence of the same nature as that of the Uranian. Let us leave to others the task of pointing out the distressing nature of such doctrine from the religious point of view. In this book I shall show its absurdity from only the scientific point of view. No doubt the beauty of the spectacle rouses a quite excusable enthusiasm when one views for the first time under the microscope one of these particles of jelly, and suddenly sees the unfolding of countless lively and interesting scenes—the long streets along which Men pass to and fro, sometimes stopping and apparently exchanging speech; or the small individual nest in which a couple keep watch over a brood of young; or armies on the march; or builders at their work. . . . But for a profitable study of the psychic faculties of these animals, it is not enough to profit by the circumstances that chance affords the observer. It is essential to know how to procure the most favorable conditions of observation, and to vary these as much as possible. It is necessary, in a word, to experiment, and thus to build up science on the solid base of fact.

This is what we have sought to do in the course of the long series of experiments reported here. Before embarking on their description I must ask the reader to imagine and to gauge the immense difficulties which such a project was bound to present. Long-distance experiment, no doubt, has become relatively easy since we had at our disposal the W rays, which enable us to grasp, handle, and even transport bodies through interstellar space. But in dealing with creatures so small and fragile as Men, the W rays are very clumsy and brutal instruments. In our first tests it turned out only too often that we killed the animals we desired to observe. Transmitting appliances of extraordinary sensitiveness were required to enable us to reach exactly the point aimed at, and to treat the sensitive matter with the necessary delicacy. In particular, when first carrying out the transference of Men from one point to another on terrestrial territory, we omitted to take full account of these animals' respiratory difficulties. We made them move too rapidly across a thin layer of air which envelops the Earth, and they died of asphyxiation. We had to construct a real box of rays, inside which the swiftness of transportation produced no effect. Similarly, when we first attempted the bisection and transference of nests, we did not make sufficient allowance for the constructional processes used by the Earth Dwellers. Experience taught us to prop up the nests after their division, by the passage of certain massive currents of rays.

The reader will find here a sketch map of that portion of the terrestrial surface on which our main experiments were carried out. We would ask him particularly to note the two great manheaps on which we made our first tests, and to which we gave the names, later adopted by the astrosociologists, of "Mad Manheap" and "Rigid Manheap."

These names we chose on account of the singularly differing plans of these manheaps, one of which at once impresses the observer by its almost geometrical star patterns of roadways, while the other is a complex maze of rather tortuous streets. Between "Mad Manheap" and "Rigid Manheap" stretches a gleaming line which is believed to be sea. The greatest manheap on the Earth is "Geometrical Manheap," which is even more regular than "Rigid Manheap"; but is far distant from the other two, and separated from them by a wider gleaming surface.

FIRST ATTEMPTS

At what point of the Earth was it best to direct our first efforts? How must we interfere with the lives of these animals in such a way as to obtain instructive reactions from them? I must confess to real emotion when I prepared for the first time to operate on the Earth, armed with an apparatus of adequate range.

I had around me four of my young pupils, who were also deeply moved, and in turn we gazed at the charming miniature landscapes in the ultratelemicroscope. Aiming the apparatus at the "Mad Man-heap," we sought a fairly open locality so as to see the consequences of our action more clearly. Tiny trees gleamed in the spring sunshine, and multitudes of small motionless insects could be seen forming irregular circles; in the middle of each of these stood an isolated insect. For a moment we speculated on the meaning of this game, but failing to find one, we decided to try an application of the rays. The effect was staggering. A hole was scooped in the ground; some of the insects were buried under the debris; and instantly an astounding activity was loosed. It really looked as if these creatures were intelligently organized. Some went to the rescue of their over-whelmed companions, others went off to get help. We then tried applying the rays on several points of the Earth, but this time we chose uninhabited areas, so as not to endanger our subjects at the very beginning of our researches. We thus learned how to reduce the power of our rays, and to operate more skillfully. Being now sure of our means of action, we decided to start the first series of our experiments.

It was my plan to take individuals in a certain man-heap, mark them with a touch of a brush, transport them to different points, and then observe whether the transported individuals would find their way back to the original manheap. At first, as I have said, we encountered great difficulties, first because the animals died during transference, and then because we had neglected to take into account the artificial epidermis with which these creatures provide themselves. They doff these coverings with the utmost ease, and so once we had set them down again in the midst of a manheap, we lost sight of them. For the subsequent transportations we tried to mark them directly on the body, tearing off the supplementary skin; but in these cases the animal made itself a new skin as soon as it arrived in the manheap.

With a little practice my assistants were at last able to follow one particular animal with the ultratelemicroscope and keep it constantly in sight. They found that in ninety-nine cases out of a hundred, the man returns to his starting point. I attempted the transference of two males from the same manheap—the "Mad Manheap"—with the extremely remote one which we termed the "Geometrical Manheap." After ten (terrestrial) days my esteemed pupil E.X. 33, who had followed them night and day with incomparable devotion, showed me them returning to the "Rigid Manheap." They had come back, notwithstanding the fact of their unfamiliarity with the places to which I had transported them; they were individuals of stay-at-home habit (we had kept them under long observation), who were obviously seeing for the first time the country where we had deposited them. How did they find the way back? Their transference had been so rapid that observation was out of the question. What was their guide? Certainly not memory, but a special faculty which we must confine ourselves to noting without claiming to explain it, so remote is it from anything in our own psychology.

These transferences raised another problem. Would the returning individual be recognized by the others? Apparently he is. Generally speaking, great excitement is to be seen in the nest when the absent one reappears. The others place their arms around him, and sometimes even place their lips on his. In certain cases, however, the feelings manifested appeared to be those of rage or displeasure.

* * *

The first experiments showed that some instinct enables Men to recognize their own manheaps. The second problem to which we turned was to find out whether, among these creatures, there existed sentiments akin to those of Uranians, and whether, for instance, conjugal or maternal love could exist on the Earth. Such an hypothesis struck me as absurd; it attributed to the Earth Dweller refinements of feeling which the Uranian has attained only through millions of years of civilization. But the duty of the experimental scientist is to approach his subject with an open mind, and to make all his experiments without any prejudice regarding their outcome.

At night the male Earth Dwelled generally rests beside his female. I asked my pupils to bisect some nests in such a way as to separate the male from the female without injuring either, and then to join up one half of Nest A with the half of Nest B, observing whether the little animals took notice of the change. For the experiment to be carried out under normal conditions, it was essential that the selected nests should closely resemble each other; and for this reason I instructed my collaborators to select two nests containing cells of the same size and broods with the same number of young. E.X. 33 showed me, not without pride, two almost identical nests in the "Mad Manheap" and the "Rigid Manheap," each of them containing a couple with four little ones. The bisection of the houses, and their transportation, were carried out with admirable skill by E.X. 33, and the results were conclusive. In both cases the couples thus artificially put together by us showed slight surprise at the moment of waking, adequately accounted for by the movement and shock. Then, in both cases. they remained together with no attempt at flight, and in apparently normal attitudes. An almost incredible fact was that, from the very first moment, each of the two females tended the other's brood with no sign of horror or distaste. They were plainly incapable of realizing that they were not dealing with their own offspring.

This experiment was repeated on numerous occasions. In 93 per cent of cases, the nests and offspring were tended by both couples. The female retains a stubborn sense of her proper functions, without having any idea of the individuals toward which she performs this duty. Whether the children are hers or not, she toils with equal fervor. It might be thought that this confusion is caused by a close resemblance between the two nests; but at different stages we chose nests of quite different appearances, joining up, for instance, the half of a shabby nest with the half of a rich nest of a different species. The results were more or less the same; Man does not distinguish between his own cell and another.

Having thus shown that in the matter of sentiment the Earth Dweller is an animal occupying a very low place in the scale of creation, we sought an appropriate means of gauging his intellectual faculties. The simplest way, it seemed to us, was to isolate a few individuals in a ray cage, and to put at their disposal food which could only be reached by means of more and more complex actions. I took particular pains to choose for this experiment certain Earth Dwellers for whom my colleague X. 38 claimed signs of scientific intelligence. In Appendix A will be found the details of this experiment. It showed beyond any possible doubt that the space of time within which Man lives is extremely limited in the past and future, that he immediately forgets, and that he is incapable of imagining the simplest method of self-preservation as soon as he is confronted by problems slightly different from those which he has, by heredity, become used to solving.

After a long period of experimenting on individual Earth Dwellers, my pupils and I became familiar enough with the movements of these animals to be able to observe them in their ordinary life without intervention on our part. It is of the utmost interest to follow, as I have done, the history of a manheap through several terrestrial years.

The origin of these human societies is unknown. Why and how did these animals abandon their freedom to become slaves of the manheap? We cannot tell. It may be that in this grouping process they found a support in warfare against other creatures and against natural forces; but it is a support for which they pay highly. No animal species is so ignorant as this one of leisure and the joy of living. In the great manheaps, and particularly the "Geometrical Manheap," activity begins at dawn and is prolonged through part of the night. Were this activity necessary, it would be comprehensible; but Man is a creature of such limited nature, so much dominated by his instincts, that he produces hardly anything beyond his requirements. Over and over again have I seen objects accumulating in the reserve stores of a manheap in such numbers that they seemed to be a source of embarrassment; and yet, only a short distance away, another group would continue to manufacture the very same objects.

Little is also known of the division of Mankind into castes. It is established that certain of these animals till the soil and produce nearly all the food-stuffs, while others make the supplementary skins or build nests, and others seem to do nothing but move swiftly to and fro over the planet's surface, eating and coupling. Why do the first two classes consent to clothe and feed the third? That remains obscure to me. E.X. 33 has written a notable thesis seeking to prove that this tolerance has a sexual origin. He has shown that at night, when the individuals of the superior caste foregather, the workers collect around the entrances to these festivities in order to see the half-nude females. According to him, the compensation of the sacrificed classes consists of the aesthetic pleasure provided by the spectacle of these easy existences. The theory strikes me as ingenious, but not so firmly based as to convince me of its truth.

For my own part, I would rather seek an explanation in Man's amazing stupidity. It is a supreme folly to be forever seeking to explain the actions of Men by Uranian reasonings. That is wrong, profoundly wrong. Man is not guided by a free intelligence. Man obeys a fatal and unconscious incitement; he cannot choose what he shall do; he slides along haphazard, following an irresistible predetermined slope which will bring him to his goal. I amused myself by following the individual existences of certain Men in whom the functions of love seemed to be the essentials of their existence. I saw how the conquest of one female to start with brought upon his shoulders all the burdens of nests and young; but, not content with that first load, my male would go off in search of a second mate, for whom he set up a new nest. These simultaneous love affairs led the wretched animal into endless battles of which I was the spectator. It mattered nothing to him; his successive woes seemed to hold no lessons for him, and he went on putting his head into his wretched adventures without seeming to be one whit the wiser after the third than after the first.

One of the strangest proofs of this inability to keep contact with the past and imagine the future was afforded me by the frightful struggles which I witnessed between individuals of one and the same species. On Uranus it would seem a grotesque idea that one group of Uranians could attack another group, hurling on it projectiles meant to injure it, and trying to asphyxiate it with poisonous gases.

That is what happened on the Earth. Within a few terrestrial years my observation showed me compact masses of men thus confronting each other, now in one corner of that planet, now in another. Sometimes they fought in the open; sometimes they crouched in earthworks and strove to demolish the adjoining earthworks by showering heavy lumps of metal on them. Note that they themselves were at the same time peppered in the same way. It is a hideous and ridiculous sight. The scenes of horror which one witnesses at these times are such that if these creatures had the slightest faculty for remembering, they would avoid their recurrence for at least several generations. But in the course of even their brief lifetimes, the same men will be seen plunging madly into the same murderous escapades.

Another striking example of this blind subservience of Man to instinct is to be seen in his habit of tirelessly rebuilding manheaps at certain points of the planet where they are fated to destruction. Thus, for instance, I have attentively watched a very populous island where, within eight years, all the nests were destroyed three times by tremors of the outer coating of the Earth. To any sensible observer it is plain that the animals living in these parts ought to migrate. They do nothing of the sort, but pick up once more, with a positively ritual action, the same pieces of wood or iron, and zealously rebuild a manheap which will once more be destroyed in the following year. But, say my critics, however absurd the goal of this activity, it remains true that the activity is regulated, and proves the existence of a directing power, a spirit. Again, a mistaken idea! The swarming of Men disturbed by an earthquake, as I have shown, resembles the movement of gaseous molecules. If the latter be observed individually, they are seen to describe irregular and complicated trajectories, but in combination their great number produces effects of decided simplicity. Similarly, if we domolish a manheap, thousands of insects collide with each other, hamper each other's movements, and show every sign of disorganized excitement; and yet, after a certain time, the manheap is discovered to be built up again.

Such is the strange intellect in which it is now fashionable to see a replica of Uranian reason! But fashion passes, facts remain; and the facts are bringing us back to the good old beliefs regarding the Uranian soul and its privileged destiny. For my own part, I shall be happy if my few experiments, modestly and prudently carried out, have helped toward the downfall of pernicious teachings, and restored these animals to their proper place in the scale of creatures. Curious and worthy of study they certainly are; but the very naïveté and incoherence of Man's behavior must force us to bear in mind how great is the gulf fixed by the Creator between bestial instinct and the Uranian soul.

DEATH OF A.E. 17

Happily, A.E. 17 died before he could witness the first interplanetary war, the establishment of relations between Uranus and the Earth, and the ruin of all his work. His great renown endured to his last days. He was a simple, kindly Uranian, who showed vexation only when contradicted. To ourselves it is an interesting fact that the monument erected to his memory on Uranus bears on its plinth a bas-relief designed from a telephotographic picture showing a swarming mass of men and women. Its background is strongly reminiscent of Fifth Avenue.

Epilogue

On the
Immortality
of the Soul
and the
Dangers
of Hasty
Conclusions

THE WEIGHER OF SOULS gives the impression of being a narrative of actual events. And, indeed, in his autobiographical sketch André Maurois tells us that he still receives inquiries from readers the world over as to whether or not the story is true. What makes it credible is first of all Maurois' superior skill as a writer. But the effect of verisimilitude is due also to its topic, which, incidentally, is one reason why this is a special kind of science fiction. For the problem of the immortality of the soul, and even the less ambitious question of temporary survival after death of our conscious personality, is not the concern of science.

As is well known, one of the main complaints the believers in survival after death make against the scientists is that they are "prejudiced" against the whole idea of the possibility of immortality and that they dismiss out of hand the so-called "paranormal" or "parapsychological" phenomena that are cited by the "immortalists" in support of their belief. There is some truth in this accusation. Thus, for example, the American biologist Hermann J. Muller, winner of the Nobel Prize, speaks in an article ("Science Fiction as an Escape," *The Humanist*, 6, December, 1957) of the "lunatic fringe" of wishful thinkers, who simply "postulate cellular intelligence or memory, vital force, perfecting principle, cosmic purpose, extrasensory perception, telepathy, telekinesis, [and] clairvoyance."

In all fairness, however, it must be stated that some prominent scientists have investigated with an open mind not only "parapsychological" phenomena but even the purported communications with the dead asserted by the spiritualists. They found the evidence wanting mainly because it did not comply with the rigorous standards of a truly scientific investigation. And apart from the unusual incidence of fraud that left even the well-intentioned scientists skeptical as to the claims of the spiritualists, it was clear that the phenomena produced by the media allow also of other explanations than that they are manifestations of the spirits of the dead.

The scientifically verified evidence of survival

after death is, nevertheless, the secret aspiration not only of the layman seeking reassurance against total annihilation but even of the scientist who does not feel that it is below his dignity to inquire into the deepest cravings of the human heart. Such was the great American psychologist and philosopher William James (1842–1910), who said that one single scientifically verified case of survival would do more for settling the dispute over the truth of immortality than all philosophical arguments put together. It is in this spirit that the problem of immortality of the soul is approached in *The Weigher of Souls* and it is perhaps no mere coincidence that the hero of Maurois' story is also called Dr. James.

One has to realize, however, that the Achilles heel of the experiments purportedly carried out by Dr. James to demonstrate survival after death are the theoretical premises on which these experiments are based. In other words, assuming that these experiments would succeed in real life, that something would escape the body at death and could be made visible by ultraviolet rays and preserved in a small glass ball, what would it prove? Maurois is careful not to make the hero of his story claim too much at the outset. He does not want to prove "the eternal survival of all personalities," only to ascertain the existence of a "vital fluid":

"I am not seeking the spirit. I am seeking a certain form of energy, which, when linked up with matter, will endow matter with that still unexplained property—life. This search does not raise the problem of the soul in the religious or philosophical sense of the word; it transposes it, it shifts it, sets it further back ... Even if I succeeded in proving that in every living being there does exist a definite mass of "vital fluid," allowance would still have to be made within the fluid itself, for spirit and matter; and then one would have to show how they are united."

As the story proceeds, however, the claim is gradually expanded: ". . . just as the soul is linked with the body for the expression of its thoughts and the perception of its sensations, so it is likewise possible that after quitting the body, it should be linked with this mysterious energy which we have just noted in the act of departure." Thus the existence of the "soul" is assumed, the possibility of its survival adumbrated, and the soul's "immortality" is restricted only in that it is predicated on preservation of the container from generation to generation.

Let us consider first the concept of a "vital fluid," or vital energy, the presence of which is supposed to make the difference between a living and a dead body. Later on, we shall consider the other assumption that there is a soul, and that if the vital energy could be made to "remain grouped in one single place," the personality could survive the body.

The notion of a "vital fluid" actually goes beyond that of vital energy, for the former is clearly "material." But since in modern physics matter and energy are interconvertible, we can disregard here this nuance. We can also disregard the Austrian physician Franz Anton Mesmer's (1734–1815) "animal magnetism," which was not so much vital energy as a mysterious force residing in himself by which he could influence others, and that, according to him, permeated the universe.

The first to assume the existence of a life force *(vis vitalis)* in order to explain the phenomena of life, and account for the difference between living things and dead matter, was probably the French philosopher Louis Dumas (1765–1813). The doctrine of "vitalism" received a severe setback when in 1828 the German chemist Friedrich Woehler succeeded in making urea in the laboratory. In spite of the vitalists' insistence that it was merely a synthesis of a "product of life," not of life itself, the materialistic position, which sought to reduce all life phenomena to physicochemical reactions, steadily gained in influence.

The materialists could point to further successes in synthetizing what until then seemed to be exclusively natural products. The discovery of "colloids" (substances that diffuse very slowly when dissolved in liquids) by the English chemist Thomas Graham (1805–1869) in 1861 further strengthened the antivitalist trend. All organisms consist largely of colloidal materials, but when it was shown that inorganic elements also form colloids, another dividing line between living and dead things collapsed. Thus the overwhelming majority of modern biologists, not to speak of biochemists and biophysicists, are firmly convinced that biological phenomena can be explained exclusively in physicochemical terms. Some confidently expect that any day now it will be possible to create life in the laboratory.

In recent times the main opposition to this mechanistic and materialistic doctrine has come from the French philosopher Henri Bergson (1859–1941) and the German biologist turned philosopher, Hans Driesch (1867–1940). Bergson's "life philosophy," which has had considerable influence on contemporary philosophical thought, sharply criticizes the natural scientist's picture of reality as grossly distorted. This is so because, according to Bergson, the intellect (intelligence) is adequate only to comprehend that part of reality that is extended and material. Therefore the other, more significant aspect of reality which is life escapes it, being misinterpreted in mechanistic terms. An organism only *seems* a mechanism when analyzed by the methods of natural science. The insight that reality is "pure duration," a "becoming" wherein the life impulse, the *élan vital,* overcomes the obstacles presented by matter comes, according to Bergson, by way of intuition.

Driesch's neo-vitalism asserts that the realm of living beings is ruled by a nonphysical, nonspatial factor that alone can account for the purposiveness so obvious in organisms. He came to this conclusion through an experiment he conducted in 1891 in which he cut the fertilized egg of a sea urchin into five parts and found that each part generated complete embryos. To explain this, he held that there must be a vital principle in each egg beyond the purely mechanical. Driesch named it "entelechy," a term coined by the Greek philosopher Aristotle and composed of three words: *en*—in, *telos*—goal, and *echein*—to have; in short, "that which has its goal in itself."

There is, however, a vast difference between Driesch's concept of entelechy and that of the old-fashioned life force. And since the former is non-material and nonspatial there can be no question of its "escaping," or its being weighed.

But the fictional Dr. James conceives the life force in even more tangible, "physical" terms than the older vitalists. He speaks of it as a "fluid" and envisages the possibility that vital energy might be conserved in analogy to the conservation of mechanical energy stipulated by the laws of thermodynamics. It is on the basis of this assumption that he undertakes his experiments, and when they seem to confirm it, he makes a further assumption of a connection between this "mysterious energy" and survival after death.

At this point the question arises as to whether the survival of the soul or conscious personality is inextricably bound up with the existence and conservation of vital energy as Dr. James presupposed.

Throughout history the soul was seen as fulfilling a double function as the source of vitality, which distinguishes living beings from "things," as well as the seat of consciousness.

The greatest philosopher of antiquity, Plato (427–347 B.C.), held that the divine and immortal soul inhabits the body like a prison, from which it is released at death. In the light of the Platonic view of the soul, Dr. James' intention of catching and preserving it in a glass ball would appear as a sacrilegious interference with the soul's divinely ordained destiny. It has to be noted, however, that the relationship between body and soul, of their essentially different "natures," creates for this so-called dualism of Plato insurmountable difficulties. How can it be united with the body and still be independent? And is it related to the body as a boatman to his boat? After two thousand years these difficulties still haunted the French philosopher René Descartes (1596–1650), the "father" of modern philosophy. Descartes assumes only "extention" (matter) and "thought" (mind or soul). The human body is part of the world of matter, and can be explained by mechanical laws. Interestingly, though, for Descartes it is not the soul that gives life to the body, for Descartes holds that death is not caused by the withdrawal of the soul, but that the immortal soul departs when at death the body becomes cold and thus "inhospitable."

While in both Plato and Descartes, the soul is a "substance" in the philosophical meaning of the word—that is, "something existing through itself and in itself, not through or in something else"—Aristotle (384–322 B.C.), the great pupil of Plato, initiates another conception of the soul. For him it is the sum of the processes of life, the active principle of organization of any living thing, the "form" of the organism. This term is understood as the factor that lends reality to a thing and sets the goal of development. As such it does not survive the body, and only the highest function of the soul, its power to think, which is of divine origin, can be said to have immortality, since at death it returns to its original source.

Christianity favors the Platonic view of the soul, although not emphasizing its extreme body-soul dualism, but the majority of philosophers and scientists incline toward the Aristotelian concept of the soul. The more radical among them consider man's mental life as an "epiphenomenon," a term coined by the English biologist Thomas Huxley (1825–1895). It means that mind or consciousness is merely a secondary phenomenon accompanying some bodily processes. This position was expressed even more bluntly by a German materialist of the nineteenth century who said that the brain generates thoughts the way the liver secretes bile; consequently, there can be no question of the mind's survival after death.

It is in order to "save the soul" that in Maurois' story Dr. James not only sees the brain in Bergsonian terms merely as a "telephone exchange" between the body and "something else" (the "soul"); he also links the soul with a hypothetical "vital force." As we have seen, however, if there be a "life-force" at all, it can be only such that its existence cannot be demonstrated by measuring devices of the laboratory. Neither can one demonstrate—because of its immateriality—the existence (let alone the survival) of "the soul," should one believe it to exist. Why, then, did Dr. James attempt an experiment which, like the construction of a perpetual-motion machine, is impossible in theory?

The main reason for his attempt was, as Maurois tells us, "his painful sense of what the irremediable cleavage of death means for human beings"—in short, this craving arises in Dr. James not out of narcissism but out of love for another human being, and death is resented because it is, to use Shakespeare's words, "love-destroying death." But for whatever reason men desire immortality, it would be unfair to denigrate this desire and to minimize the emotional and intellectual "disquietude" connected with the fear of mortality. Where it is considerable, only the belief in the continuation of our conscious personality beyond death can appease it.

Since the success of the experiment in *The Weigher of Souls* is fiction, it seems appropriate to conclude this discussion with some of the arguments that have been advanced in support of the belief in the immortality of the soul.

Plato has presented several, among which is the assertion that all true knowledge is recollection. But this would prove only the pre-existence of the soul, not its continuous existence after death. According to Plato, however, true knowledge is knowledge of eternal "forms" or "ideas" and since "nothing mortal can know what is immortal," the soul itself must be immortal. Another of Plato's "proofs" is that the soul is "simple"—that is, it cannot be divided in parts, and therefore it is indestructible. This argument has been extensively used in later times and has become known as the "ontological proof."

The so-called theological argument is that God's intentions in creating conscious persons cannot be fulfilled in the brief span of their earthly existence and that therefore there must be an afterlife. The specifically Christian argument is the Resurrection of Christ and His promise of life eternal to all men who believe in Him. The moral argument, in its more popular form, is that since bad deeds are not always punished and good deeds are not always rewarded in this life, true justice requires that there should be another life to carry it out. The German philosopher Immanuel Kant's (1724–1804) famous argument for immortality is similar: We are required by moral law to be perfect. An obligation is invalid, unless it can be fulfilled, and since moral perfection is unattainable in this life, immortality is "a postulate of practical reason." Finally, the historical argument is the purported universality of the belief in immortality.

It is interesting that Maurois himself is not convinced by any of the arguments. In a little book called *What I Believe,* and published a quarter of a century after *The Weigher of Souls,* he writes: "I do not know whether any part of us survives our body. It seems to me quite improbable that personal consciousness continues after the ruin of our senses. . . ." And in adding that, "Be it as it may, I do not fear death," he admonishes that, "It is necessary to live as if we were eternal; which is true for every one of us, but only for himself."

The other story in this volume, *The Earth Dwellers,* shows us a "fantastic" and improbable series of events that, ironically enough, is presented as an actual study of earth men by an observer on the planet Uranus. It is, as Maurois himself points out, "a satire of hasty conclusions." It contains a moral that also has considerable bearing on the problem dealt with in *The Weigher of Souls.* For a truly objective mind would have to admit that the categorical denial as well as the categorical assertion of survival after death must both be, so far, considered as a hasty conclusion, as must the Uranian observer's categorical denial of human intelligence or our denial of the existence of Uranians. In the last resort emotional and cultural factors determine whether preference is given to the one or the other alternative. But this is often the case with nonmetaphysical matters as well. The English philosopher Sir Francis Bacon (1561–1626) was the first to call attention to the obstacles standing in the way of true knowledge that he called "idols." He distinguished four kinds: some are grounded in human nature, some are due to individual preferences, others again are due to the theories prevailing at the time, and, the most dangerous of all are the pitfalls of language, when words used in everyday discourse are employed indiscriminately. Bacon's theory of the "idols" implies, however, that these obstacles can be eliminated, whereas the modern "sociology of knowledge" is less confident in this respect. Influenced by, but not necessarily sold on, the German thinker Karl Marx's (1818–1883) theory that all knowledge is inextricably bound up with the individual's belonging to either the class of the "exploiters" or to that of the "exploited," it studies those social processes that may have an influence on knowledge.

The questions of whether only the social and not also the "psychological" processes should be considered and whether all knowledge, or only such realms of knowledge where the human factor is prominently involved, are affected, make for an important and fascinating study. Its relevance becomes particularly clear when we deal with such topics as the mentality of primitive peoples or the "psychology" of animals, in particular with those closest to us on the evolutionary scale. As the English philosopher and mathematician Bertrand Russell has pointedly remarked in connection with the latter, animals behave in a manner showing the rightness of the views of the man who observes them. And what Maurois tells us about the conclusions to which inhabitants of other planets might come about us applies also to our own speculations about these denizens of outer space. It is also a warning that should we ever come to pay *them* a visit, we had better not jump to hasty conclusions about their feelings, desires, and thoughts.

Jacques Choron

Bibliography

The
Works
of André
Maurois

1920

Les Bourgeois de Witzheim
("The Bourgeois of Witz-
heim")

1922

*Les Discours du Docteur
O'Grady*
("The Discourses of Doctor
O'Grady")

1923

Ariel, ou la Vie de Shelley
("Ariel, or The Life of
Shelley")

Ariel, A Shelley Romance. Translated by Ella d'Arcy. London: J.
Lane, Ltd., 1924; New York: Appleton-Century-Crofts, 1924, 1925, 1930.

1924

*Dialogues sur le Com-
mandement*
("Dialogues on Leader-
ship")

*Captains and Kings; Three Dia-
logues on Leadership.* Translated by
J. Lewis May. New York: Appleton-
Century-Crofts, 1925.

*Essais sur la Littérature
Anglaise*
("Essays on English Litera-
ture")

1925

Portrait d'une Actrice
("Portrait of an Actress")

1926

Bernard Quesnay
("Bernard Quesnay")

Bernard Quesnay. Translated by
Brian W. Downs. New York: Appleton-Century-Crofts, 1927.

Une Carrière
("A Quarry")

Meipe, ou la Délivrance
("Mape, or the Deliver-
ance")

Mape; The World of Illusion.
Translated by Eric Sutton. New
York: Appleton-Century-Crofts,
1926.

1927

Les Anglais
("The English")

Conseils à un Jeune Fran-çais Partant pour l'Angle-terre ("Advice to a Young French-man Leaving for England")	In *A Private Universe*
La Conversation ("Conversation")	*Conversation.* Translated by Yvonne Dufour. New York: E. P. Dutton and Company, Inc., 1930.
Un Essai sur Dickens ("An Essay on Dickens")	*Dickens.* Translated by Hamish Miles. London: John Lane, 1934; New York and London: Harper and Row, 1935.
Études Anglaises ("English Studies")	
Rouen ("Rouen")	
La Vie de Disraeli ("The Life of Disraeli")	*Disraeli; A Picture of the Victorian Age.* Translated by Hamish Miles. New York: Appleton-Century-Crofts, 1928.
Voyage au Pays des Arti-coles ("A Voyage to the Country of the Articoles")	*A Voyage to the Island of the Articoles.* Translated by David Garret. London: J. Cape, 1928; New York: Appleton-Century-Crofts, 1929.
1928	
Aspects de la Biographie ("Aspects of Biography")	*Aspects of Biography.* Translated by S. C. Roberts. New York: Appleton-Century-Crofts, 1929.
Climats ("Climates")	*Atmosphere of Love.* Translated by Joseph Collins. New York: Apple-ton-Century-Crofts, 1929. *The Cli-mates of Love.* Translated by Violet Schiff and Esme Cook. London: Barrie, 1957.
Le Pays des Trente-six Mille Volontés ("The Country of Thirty-Six Thousand Wishes")	*The Country of Thirty-Six Thou-sand Wishes.* Translated by Pauline Fairbanks. Illustrated by Adrienne Segur. New York: Appleton-Cen-tury-Crofts, 1930.

1929

Fragments d'un Journal de Vacances
("Fragments of a Vacation Diary")

In *A Private Universe*

Le Roman et le Romancier
("The Novel and The Novelist")

Le Coté de Chelsea
("Chelsea Way")

Chelsea Way. Translated by Hamish Miles. London: E. Matthews and Marrot, 1930.

Les Mondes Imaginaires
("Imaginary Worlds")

1930

Byron

Byron. Translated by Hamish Miles. New York: Appleton-Century-Crofts, 1930; New York: Grosset and Dunlap, 1956.

Patapoufs et Filifers
("Patapoufs and Filifers")

Fattypuffs and Thinifers. Translated by Norman Denny. Illustrated by Jean Bruller. London: John Lane, 1941. *Patapoufs and Filifers*. With introduction, notes, exercises, and vocabulary by Mary E. Storer. Boston: D. C. Heath, 1948.

1931

L'Amérique Inattendue
("America The Unexpected")

In *A Private Universe*

Lyautey

Lyautey. Translated by Hamish Miles. New York: Appleton-Century-Crofts, 1931.

Le Peseur d'Âmes
("The Weigher of Souls")

The Weigher of Souls. Translated by Hamish Miles. New York and London: Appleton-Century-Crofts, 1931.

Tourgueniev
("Turgenev")

1932

L'Anglaise et d'Autres Fem-mes
("Englishwomen and Other Women")

Ricochets; Miniature Tales of Human Life. Translated by Hamish Miles. New York and London: Harper and Row, 1935.

Le Cercle de Famille
("The Family Circle")

The Family Circle. Translated by Hamish Miles. New York: Appleton-Century-Crofts, 1932.

Voltaire

Voltaire. Translated by Hamish Miles. New York: Appleton-Century-Crofts, 1932.

A Private Universe. Translated by Hamish Miles. New York: Appleton-Century-Crofts, 1932.

1933

Chantiers Américains
("American Shipyards")

Edouard VII et Son Temps
("Edward VII and His Times")

King Edward and His Times. Translated by Hamish Miles. London: Cassell and Company, Ltd., 1933. *The Edwardian Era.* Translated by Hamish Miles. New York: Appleton-Century-Crofts, 1936.

Introduction á la Méthode de Paul Valéry
("Introduction To The Method of Paul Valery")

Mes Songes Que Voici . . .
("Here Are My Dreams")

1934

L'Instinct du Bonheur
("The Instinct of Happiness")

A Time For Silence. Translated by Edith Johannsen. New York and London: Appleton-Century-Crofts, 1942.

1935

Magiciens et Logiciens
("Magicians and Logicians")
Sentiments et Coutumes
("Sentiments and Customs")

1936

Londres
("London")

1937

Histoire d'Angleterre
("History of England")

La Jeunesse devant Notre Temps
La Machine à Lire les Pensées
("The Thought-Reading Machine")

1938

Chateaubriand

Un Art de Vivre
("An Art of Living")

Discours de Réception
("Discourse on Reception")
États-Unis 1939. Journal d'un Voyage en Amérique.
("The United States, 1939. Diary of a Voyage in America")

The Miracle of England. Translated by Hamish Miles. London: J. Cape, 1937. *A History of England.* Translated by Hamish Miles. Rev. ed., New York: Grove Press, 1960.

The Thought-Reading Machine. Translated by Hamish Miles. New York and London: Harper and Row, 1935.

Chateaubriand, Poet, Statesman, Lover. Translated by Vera Fraser. New York and London: Harper and Row, 1938.

The Art of Living. Translated by James Whitall. New York and London: Harper and Row, 1940. Second ed., 1960.

1940

Tragédie en France
("Tragedy in France")

Tragedy in France. Translated by Denver Lindley. New York and London: Harper and Row, 1940.

1941

Défense de la France
("The Defense of France")

The Battle of France. Translated by F. R. Ludman. London: J. Lane, The Bodley Head, 1940.

Études Littéraires
("Literary Studies")

1942

Sept Visages de l'Amour
("Seven Faces of Love")

Seven Faces of Love. Translated by Haakon M. Chevalier. New York: Didier, 1944.

Mémoires. Tome I: *Les Années d'Apprentissage.* Tome II: *Les Années de Travail*
("Memoirs. Volume I: The Years of Apprenticeship. Volume II: The Years of Work")

Histoire des États-Unis. Tome I: 1492-1828. Tome II: 1828-1940
("History of the United States")

The Miracle of America. Translated by Denver and June Lindley. New York and London: Harper and Row, 1944.

Toujours l'Inattendu Arrive
("The Unexpected Always Arrives")

La Vie de Disraeli
("The Life of Disraeli")

Disraeli. New York: Modern Library, 1942.

1944

Études Littéraires
("Literary Studies")

1945

Eisenhower

Eisenhower, the Liberator. Drawings by George Avison. Translated by Eileen Lane Kinney. New York: Didier, 1945.

Franklin

Franklin, the Life of an Optimist. Drawings by Howard Simon. Translated by Howard Simon. New York: Didier, 1945.

Terre Promise
("Promised Land")

Woman without Love. Translated by Gerard Hopkins. New York: Harper and Row, 1945.

1946

Études Américaines
("American Studies")

Journal. États-Unis 1946
("Diary. United States 1946")

From My Journal. Translated by John Charles. New York: Harper and Row, 1948.

Washington

Washington, the Life of a Patriot. Illustrated by Henry C. Pitz. Translated by Eileen Lane Kinney. New York: Didier, 1946.

Conseil à un Jeune Français Partant pours les États-Unis
("Advice to a Young Frenchman Leaving for the United States")

In *A Private Universe*

Histoire de la France
("History of France")

The Miracle of France. Translated by Henry L. Binsse. New York: Harper and Row, 1948.

Retour en France
("Return to France")

1948

Journal d'un Tour en Amérique Latine.

My Latin-American Diary. Translated by Frank Jackson. London:

("Diary of a Tour in Latin America")	Falcon Press, 1953.
Journal d'un Tour en Suisse ("Diary of a Tour in Switzerland")	
Rouen Devasté ("Rouen Devastated")	

1949

À la Recherche de Marcel Proust ("The Search for Marcel Proust")	*Proust: Portrait of a Genius.* Translated by Gerard Hopkins, New York: Harper and Row, 1950.

Alain

1950

Nouveaux Discours du Docteur O'Grady ("New Discourse on Doctor O'Grady")	*The Return of Doctor O'Grady.* Translated by Gerard Hopkins. London: Bodley Head, 1951.

1951

Le Diner sous les Marronniers
("The Dinner under the Chestnut Trees")

Cours de Bonheur Conjugal ("The Course of Happy Marriage")	*The Art of Being Happily Married.* Translated by Crystal Herbert. New York: Harper and Row, 1953.

Paris

1952

Lélia ou la Vie de George Sand ("Lélia or The Life of George Sand")	*Lélia, The Life of George Sand.* Translated by Gerard Hopkins. New York: Harper and Row, 1953

Ce Que Je Crois
("What I Believe")

1953

L'Angleterre Romantique
("The English Romantics")

Lettres à l'Inconnue
("Letters to an Unknown
Woman")

1954

Olympio ou la Vie de Victor Hugo
("Olympio or The Life of
Victor Hugo")

Versailles aux Lumières
("Versailles Illuminated")

1955

*Aux Innocents les Mains
Pleines*
("Dumb Luck")

Hollande
("Holland")

Robert et Elizabeth Browning
("Robert and Elizabeth
Browning")

Périgord

*Discours Prononcés dans
La Séance du Jeudi 20
Octobre 1955, pour La Réception de Jean Cocteau
l'Académie Française*
("Lecture at the Meeting
of Thursday October 20,
1955, for the Reception of
Jean Cocteau into the
French Academy")

To an Unknown Lady. Translated
by John Buchanan-Brown. New
York: Dutton, 1957.

Cecil Rhodes. New York: The Macmillan Company, 1953.

Olympio: The Life of Victor Hugo.
Translated by Gerard Hopkins.
New York: Harper and Row, 1956.

A Vision of Versailles. Translated by
A. S. Alexander Brionne. N. C.:
Amelot, 1955.

1956

Les Roses de Septembre
("September Roses")

September Roses. Translated by Gerard Hopkins. New York: Harper and Row, 1958.

La France Change de Visage
("The Changing Face of France")

1957

Les Trois Dumas
("The Three Dumas")

The Titans, A Three-Generation Biography of the Dumas. Translated by Gerard Hopkins. New York: Harper and Row, 1957.

Lecture Mon Doux Plaisir
("On my Sweet Pleasure")

The Art of Writing. Translated by Gerard Hopkins. New York: Dutton, 1960.

The French Boy. With photographs by Gerard Maurois. New York: Sterling Publishing Company, 1957.

1958

Louis XIV à Versailles
("Louis XIV in Versailles")

1959

La Vie de Sir Alexander Fleming
("The Life of Sir Alexander Fleming")

The Life of Sir Alexander Fleming, Discoverer of Penicillin. Translated by Gerard Hopkins. New York: E. P. Dutton, 1959.

Dialogues des Vivants
("Dialogues on Living")

Adrienne, ou la Vie de Madame de La Fayette
("Adrienne, or The Life of Lady de La Fayette")

Adrienne: The Life of the Marquise de La Fayette. Translated by Gerard Hopkins. New York: McGraw-Hill, 1961.

Pour Piano Seul
("For Solo Piano")

1960

Le Monde de Marcel Proust ("The World of Marcel Proust")	*Proust: A Biography.* Translated by Gerard Hopkins. New York: Meridian Books, 1960.
	Lafayette in America. Illustrated by Frank Nicholas. Boston: Houghton Mifflin, 1960.

ANDRÉ MAUROIS BOOKS IN PRINT

Alexandre Dumas. New York: Knopf, 1955.

Ariel: The Life of Shelley. New York: F. Ungar Publishing Company, 1952.

The Art of Being Happily Married. New York: Harper and Row, 1956.

The Art of Living. New York: Harper and Row, 1959.

The Art of Writing. New York: E. P. Dutton and Company, 1960.

Cecil Rhodes. New York: The Macmillan Company, 1953.

Chateaubriand. New York: Harper and Row, 1959.

Disraeli. New York: Modern Library, 1942.

The French Boy. New York: Sterling Publishing Company, Inc., 1957.

The History of England. New York: Farrar, Straus and Cudahy, Inc., 1958; Rev. ed., New York: Grove Press, Inc., 1960 (paperback).

The History of France. New York: Farrar, Straus and Cudahy, 1957; New York: Grove Press, Inc., 1960.

The Illustrated History of France. New York: Viking Press, 1960.

Lafayette in America. Boston: Houghton, Mifflin and Company, 1960.

Lélia: The Life of George Sand. New York: Harper and Row, 1953.

The Life of Sir Alexander Fleming. New York: E. P. Dutton and Company, 1959.

Olympio: The Life of Victor Hugo. New York: Harper and Row, 1956.

Proust: A Biography. New York: Meridian Books, 1960 (paperback).

The Titans. New York: Harper and Row, 1958.

To An Unknown Lady. New York: E. P. Dutton and Company, 1957.

ABOUT THE COMMENTATOR

JACQUES CHORON, born in Russia, received his Ph.D. from Leipzig University, Germany. Now a resident of New York City, he received his D.S.Sc. from New York's New School for Social Research where he lectures in philosophy. Among his most recent works are *Death and Western Thought* and *The Romance of Philosophy*.

ABOUT THE ILLUSTRATOR

LEONARD EVERETT FISHER has illustrated over seventy books, including a number in the field of science; three of these he has written himself. A native of New York, he studied art at the Hecksher Foundation, the Art Students League, and the studio of Moses and Raphael Soyer. He was awarded the Pulitzer Art Prize in 1950. Mr. Fisher has also illustrated *Before Adam* and *The Star Rover* in Macmillan's Library of Science Fiction Classics.

The Weigher of Souls
&
The Earth Dwellers
BY ANDRÉ MAUROIS

Translated from the French by Hamish Miles

Autobiographical Introduction

Epilogue by Jacques Choron

Illustrated by Leonard Everett Fisher

The eminent French author and member of the French Academy, André Maurois, has applied his skill as a storyteller to science fiction and has produced two tales of suspense and irony.

Determined to find a way to preserve the soul, a London doctor in *The Weigher of Souls* succeeds in his extraordinary attempt and shares the secret with a friend who narrates the story. It is told so convincingly that readers continue to inquire of Maurois if the story is true. The author has called this short novel his favorite, and this preference was shared by his distinguished colleague, André Gide.

In *The Earth Dwellers,* a "satire on hasty conclusions," the fictitious inhabitants of Uranus carry on experiments with the people on earth, whom they have been observing through "celestial ultra-microscopes." Looking down at them as though at ants, the Uranian scientists study the earthlings' reactions to the accidents to which they are subjected. From these studies, the Uranians conclude that mankind is motivated entirely by instinct and, unlike them, is not endowed with the higher faculties of intelligence and moral sensibilities.